A timeless discovery...

The next time Shade lowered his head to touch her lips, Lori found the strength she lacked a moment ago. Her arms went around his waist. Lori was the one with the need to press their bodies together, to feel his muscular legs against her thighs, to know the mixture of pleasure and wanting that came from removing the layers of fabric separating them. Shade was like a rock, a mass of granite that formed the perfect contrast to her own slight frame.

So this was what was good about being small. For maybe the first time in her life, Lori found nothing wrong with her soft womanly body. Maybe it wasn't capable of doing all the physical chores she wanted from it. But it was perfect for molding against this man's body.

ABOUT THE AUTHOR

Vella Munn claims she has only one pseudonym—Mom. Originally from California, she now resides in Oregon with her husband and two sons. Before turning to writing full-time, Vella penned more than fifty articles and a nonfiction book, and worked as a reporter and a social worker.

Books by Vella Munn

HARLEQUIN AMERICAN ROMANCE

HARLEQUIN INTRIGUE

These books may be available at your local bookseller.

Don't miss any of our special offers. Write to us at the following address for information on our newest releases.

Harlequin Reader Service
P.O. Box 52040, Phoenix, AZ 85072-2040
Canadian address: P.O. Box 2800, Postal Station A,
5170 Yonge St., Willowdale, Ont. M2N 6J3

Wanderlust

VELLA MUNN

Harlequin Books

TORONTO • NEW YORK • LONDON
AMSTERDAM • PARIS • SYDNEY • HAMBURG
STOCKHOLM • ATHENS • TOKYO • MILAN

Published August 1985

First printing June 1985

ISBN 0-373-16115-8

Printed in Canada

Chapter One

Rain, a heavy mist really, had settled around the valley, closing Lori Black off from everything except her thoughts. Because the day had been warm, Lori still wore the sleeveless T-shirt and twill slacks she'd driven in, but now that she'd been standing outside the farm property for five minutes, her clothes were penetrated by moisture. The pale blue T-shirt clung to her breasts and rib cage; her short dark hair glistened. Lori absently brushed damp hair away from her forehead and pushed away from the old Mustang she'd been leaning against.

There weren't any signs to identify the Kadin ranch, but Lori had seen pictures of the place and she wasn't mistaken. The two-story white frame house was barely visible through the jungle of trees and overgrown shrubbery; the massive barn to the left looked as if it was listing to one side; a rusting piece of farm machinery sat mired in the middle of a nearly mature wheat field. Because it had been dark for over an hour, Lori couldn't identify the various species of plants that ringed the ranch house like a green wall, but she'd wanted to come here as soon as she reached the valley.

I've got to be prepared tomorrow, Lori thought. *At least I can say I've been out here.*

She stepped hesitantly up to the open gate leading into the winding private drive. There weren't any Keep Off signs, but she still didn't feel right about walking right in, especially at night like this. She thought about going up to the house and introducing herself but hesitated. According to the information she had on the Kadin ranch, an elderly woman lived alone here. It might frighten her to have a stranger show up on her doorstep on a moonless, misting northwest night.

Lori's thoughts were interrupted by the sound of something padding along the wet gravel toward her. She stiffened, recognizing the sound as coming from a dog but having no idea whether the dog was friendly or not. She heard the animal's breathing long before she was able to make out the dark bundle of fur with a tail wagging so enthusiastically that the animal hit its side with every wag.

"You're a great watchdog, aren't you?" Lori asked as she knelt down to receive a wet bundle in her arms. The dog's front paws raked her thighs and left mud tracks on her pants, but Lori barely noticed. It had been a long time since she'd been accepted uncompromisingly by a living creature. "Hi, fella. Do you have a name? You're wetter than I am. You know that?"

As if the dog understood what was being said, it squirmed and wriggled until its nose was buried tightly against Lori's side. It breathed loudly through its nose, the first true sound Lori had heard since she stepped into the mist. She hugged the dog back, not denying the flood of emotion that swept through her. She missed Zero more than she thought possible. The red male mutt she'd brought home from the Humane Society had been her one confidant during the months before her divorce. "What do you think?" Lori asked the wet black bundle. "Do you think Mrs. Kadin is going to have a heart attack if I ring her doorbell?"

Unfortunately, the dog didn't seem capable of imparting that kind of information. With a sigh Lori rose to her feet, brushed absently at her slacks and started tentatively up the crushed-rock drive. Vines and low-hanging branches from several massive oak trees threatened to block off her path, but at least they provided some kind of protection from the softly falling rain. Lori shivered once, but she wasn't cold enough to go back to her car for some kind of wrap. Besides, the mist was promising purification. She stopped for a moment when there was a break in the shrubbery and lifted her head. The clouds hanging low over the valley were more gray than black, a friendly blanket designed to wash away dust but not enough to swell the creeks.

Lori felt moisture on her eyelashes, forehead and lips, accepting the cool penetration. It took her back to a fall she'd spent on the Oregon coast with her father when fog and mist seemed to begin and end every day. Black Bob would like this place. The acreage around the farm was large enough to keep neighbors at more than arm's length. In fact, except for the strangely listing barn, Lori couldn't see any other buildings. That was how Black Bob liked things. "People live jammed up next to other people" was as close as he ever came to philosophy. "That's what's wrong with the world. There's no elbow room. Makes people nervous to have other people living in their pockets."

There certainly wouldn't be a problem with neighbors sticking their elbows up next to Mrs. Kadin, Lori thought as she started walking again, choosing her steps carefully because the little black dog was underfoot. A thought warmed her. Her father, Black Bob, would feel at home here. It made her wonder if the elderly lady who lived here ever got lonely, whether it was safe for her to live clear out here.

That's not what you're here for, she chided herself. *You want to sound knowledgeable tomorrow. Take a look at what's around you.*

That was easier said than done. There was no way she'd be able to identify what kind of vines were climbing over the edges of the gravel road seemingly in defiance of automobile traffic, and she had no way of knowing what was healthy or unhealthy growth overhead. Maybe the most she'd be able to tell whoever was going to interview her was that a lot of pruning had to be done in order to allow the sun to penetrate the thick foliage. Obviously, many years had passed since any of the trees had had any attention.

Suddenly, the little dog left Lori's feet and catapulted its body forward. Its movement was accompanied by a loud chorus of happy barks. Lori stopped. She wondered if the elderly woman was out here, but she was afraid that anything she'd say would startle her.

"Hello out there. Stand and identify yourself." The voice was masculine, strong and confident.

"Hello," Lori replied, feeling embarrassed, startled and self-conscious. The hair on the back of her neck rose; meeting a man wasn't the most comforting thought. She had no idea what he was doing here. "I— the dog said I was welcome."

"This mutt would welcome Jack the Ripper. You haven't come to steal the family jewels, have you? I'm afraid you're going to be disappointed. There isn't much except some old furniture that's too heavy for you to throw over your shoulder."

At that Lori relaxed. Despite the deep tone of his

voice, the man didn't sound menacing. "I'm sorry," she continued. "I left my car back at the gate. I hope I didn't startle anyone."

"Not really. I heard the car. You have muffler problems."

Lori laughed. Talking to this stranger was so easy. "That's not the only problem that old relic has. Ah, I know it's late, but I wonder if Mrs. Kadin would mind if I looked around."

The man stepped out of the shadows. Lori could make out glinting, thick curled hair. He was wearing a T-shirt that looked as wet as hers, but because it was dark, she couldn't hazard a guess at his age within twenty years. His silhouette was tall and broad enough that she quickly dismissed the thought that he might be Mrs. Kadin's age. Besides, his strong voice didn't belong to an old man. "I doubt if she'd mind," he said. "But Ruth went to bed about a half hour ago. When you're eighty-five, you need all the beauty rest you can get."

"Oh." Lori started to form an explanation for why she was here but stopped herself. The man certainly was big. His frame seemed to blend in with the night, making it hard for Lori to determine where he left off and the surroundings began. She wasn't sure how much of herself she wanted to reveal to this wet, impressive stranger. "I guess I should come back in the morning," she finished instead.

"Is it something I can help you with?" he asked, inclining his head toward her. "Ruth lets me pretend I have some say around here. You aren't lost, are you?"

Lori shook her head and brushed wet bangs away from her forehead. "No." She'd never pretended to have any so-called women's intuition, but something told her she had nothing to fear physically from this man. "Actually, why I'm here is kind of complicated. Is—well, I was going to ask Mrs. Kadin if I could familiarize myself with the place."

"In the rain? You're soaking wet."

Lori glanced down at herself. He was right. There wasn't much left to the imagination. Thanks to the mist, her sleeveless top clung to her like a second skin. There was no way she could hide the fact that the cold night air had hardened her nipples. She must look like a waif or someone who decided to take a leave of absence from the state mental hospital. She had no idea what she could say or do to convince him that she didn't need a keeper. "I like the rain," she said lamely. "I've been in a car all day. It's almost as good as a shower."

"Most people take off their clothes when they take a shower." He smiled. "You're going to get cold."

This was ridiculous. Grown people don't stand in the middle of what looks like a jungle talking about taking showers when it's too dark for them to have any idea what the other looks like. "I'll be going to a motel soon," Lori said, because she couldn't think of anything else. "I'm sorry. I didn't mean to disturb anyone." She took a tentative step backward.

"Hey, don't run off." The man reached out and touched Lori's shoulder but didn't hold on to her. "Ruth would have my hide if I wasn't friendly to her visitors. You said you wanted to look around. Is there anything I can help you with?"

"I don't know." For some reason the man's touch had a settling effect on her nerves. She no longer felt embarrassed. In fact, what she felt was very human and warm. It made it easier to remember why she'd come here. "It certainly is overgrown. How long has it been since anyone has done any work on the yard?"

"At least twenty years. I don't know how much you know about the Kadin family, but William Kadin died in the sixties. Ruth has carried on alone since then. She's had some help with the crops, but the yard has really been neglected. That's going to be turned around now."

Lori nodded. She understood the plans for the ranch. That had been included in the lengthy letter from the historical society. What impressed her was how much the man knew. Obviously he hadn't just been wandering around tonight. "Are you a relative? How much do you know about the historical society? I'm sorry." Lori clamped a hand over her mouth. "This is ridiculous. I'm asking all these questions, and I haven't even told you who I am."

"That was going to be my question," the man supplied, glancing up as if trying to determine whether something was going to drop on his head. "Who are you?"

Lori stuck out a wet hand. "Lori Jordan, ah, Black. Lori Black."

"Hello, Lori Jordan Black. I'm Shade Ryan. And don't ask me about the name. I have no idea why my parents named me Shade. My mother always told me to ask my father, and my father said he'd forgotten."

Lori laughed. Her laughter carried her past the experience of having her hand smothered in a wet one big enough to crush her fingers if he wasn't careful. "That sounds like my father," she said. "His name is Robert Black, but he's been Black Bob since he was a kid." It wasn't until Lori's hand had been released that she realized she'd just told this stranger something she hadn't told more than two or three other people.

"Our fathers should get together. It sounds as if they have a lot in common."

"Sorry. I don't even know where Black Bob is right now. Maybe—" she said lamely, and quickly returned to her earlier question. "Are you related to Mrs. Kadin?"

Shade Ryan shrugged, and for a moment the movement mesmerized Lori. There was no denying that this man was all male.

"She wouldn't have me," he was saying in a voice strong enough to take her thoughts with him. "Says I don't know enough about farming to keep a rabbit from starving. She's right, but then we all have our niches in life. You know about the historical society?"

"A little." Lori shifted her feet. Her tennis shoes were getting wet and chilling her feet. She wasn't going to be able to stand out here much longer. "I hope to be working for the society. Can you tell me anything about it?"

"I suppose I could, but I don't want to. You see, I work for the society, and it's after hours. It's a good job—don't get me wrong—but this isn't the time or place for shop talk. What if I give you the budget tour? That's all I have time for and about all you can stand if you don't want to risk getting sick. I'm afraid we're both going to be locked up for demonstrating blatant incompetence if we don't get out of the rain pretty soon."

Lori hung back from accepting Shade Ryan's offer. He sounded friendly enough, but she couldn't shake the feeling that they were the only two people outside tonight. Besides, the truth of the matter was that she was unable to shake his decidedly masculine image. The misting rain had settled down around them like a thick fog, cutting them off from lights and roads and telephones, isolating them from all signs of civilization. While she was alone, Lori hadn't minded the night rain, but she wasn't alone anymore. Finding someone like him out here was almost more than her senses could deal with. Learning that he worked for the historical society didn't dull what she felt.

As if he could read her thoughts, Shade took a step backward. "I promise you I won't bite. Look, Fang thinks I'm all right. Would he lie?"

Lori had to laugh. She couldn't very well call the wet, muddy dog a liar. "No. I just don't want to inconvenience you."

"I'd be a lot more inconvenienced if I drove off and left you out here alone. I have a habit of picking up strays. I can't seem to break myself of that."

Lori might have imagined it, but she thought there was a certain resignation, a distress, even in Shade's admission. She couldn't help but wonder if he thought of her as a stray. Lori would have liked to be able to deny that, but she couldn't. She felt like an outcast these days. "Do you know what kinds of plantings are around the place?" she asked in an attempt to steer the conversation in a safe direction. "That's what I really need to know."

"I don't know poison oak from an oak tree. That's why Ruth won't adopt me. But I do know my way around here without getting lost. Will that do?"

Before Lori had time to answer, Shade placed his arm over her shoulder and was leading her down the narrow, foliage-framed road. She felt masculine muscle, hard sinew. A frame like that took work to develop.

And maybe effort to control once developed. If it wasn't for the civilized impact of his after-shave, she would have had even more trouble remembering that this was an intelligent, articulate man instead of some primitive creature spawned from her restless, lonely nights. She had to duck her head to prevent being slapped in the face by a low-hanging branch. Shade used his free arm to push away another limb. "You're right," he said softly. "It is a jungle here. About all this place lacks is Tarzan swinging through the trees."

Ground cover of some kind that reached almost waist high was scraping past her pants. She had to lean close to Shade to keep from being tripped up. She could only hope he didn't know how hard it was to concentrate on anything except his body so close to hers. "Where are we going?" she managed.

"To my favorite spot. You know what a springhouse is, don't you?"

"I think so." Lori grimaced as a thorny bush caught her ankle. "Is there one here?"

"Yep. It's in here somewhere. The ivy has just about swallowed it, but we might be able to find it." Shade pushed Lori behind him as he picked his way through their junglelike surroundings, somehow finding a narrow path in the sloping ground. "It's a good thing Ruth doesn't need to come here for her water. She's too independent for her own good. Someday she's going to get hurt if she doesn't watch herself."

Lori started to ask if Shade was some kind of caretaker for the woman who lived here. That's when she was able to make out the barest outline of a low rock building settled in a depression in the ground. A tree seemed to be growing horizontally practically into the building, and she couldn't tell where the door was. If it was daylight, Lori probably wouldn't resist the urge to climb the tree and scramble onto the low roof. Probably break her foot when the wooden, moss-covered roof gave way. "That's the springhouse?"

"That's it. Ruth's father built it when they first moved here. They used it as a root cellar for years. There's a natural underground spring here. Clearest, coldest water in the county. The Kadin farm is like walking into the past. A link I hope we never lose."

Lori stared up at Shade. His arm was still around her, holding her protectively against his hard, damp side. She dropped the idea that he might be Ruth's guardian. A historian, maybe.

His comment about the past had been spoken with reverence, as if he shared what she was feeling. He was right. Because there were no streetlights, no moon to break the night, they seemed to be standing in a spot without time. The years, the hours even, didn't have anything to do with them.

The thought engulfed Lori and left her without the power of speech. She was a child again, a young girl trailing after her father as he pushed through a forest on their way to a logging operation. The trees towering over her were ageless. They knew nothing of wars in foreign countries, automobiles, man's dreams of pushing into space. The forest swallowed the little girl and left her rootless somewhere between prehistoric past and the future. Here the time span wasn't as great, but the impact on her senses was just as effective. This was one of those rare, special moments to be savored and then locked away, protected by the heart.

"I hope we never lose that link," Lori found herself saying. She found herself fighting a wave of emotion that wanted to break all the rules and give her the gall to reach up and claim Shade Ryan's lips. Wondering if she'd discovered a man with emotions that equaled hers was doing things to her senses that she couldn't try to explain. "At least there's security in the past," she said to silence her thoughts. "We know what it holds."

She could feel Shade staring down at her and wasn't sure that she'd been able to keep her primitive emotion to herself. "That's a profound statement coming from a young woman," he whispered. "Do you feel more comfortable with the past?"

She wasn't going to answer that question. This man, this stranger, wasn't privy to her thoughts. It was just her shock at feeling this way that made her feel naked emotionally. Her hands weren't on his body. He couldn't know that that's where she wanted to place them. "I'm not sure I feel comfortable with anything," she whispered, regretting her comment before she'd finished speaking the words. "I—I guess I'm getting too cold to be able to concentrate on anything," she amended quickly, her eyes still drawn to the cold outlines of the springhouse. She fixed her thoughts on images of preserved fruits and vegetables stored for the winter inside the cool darkness.

Shade shrugged, taking her slight body with his movement. "I'll accept that, for tonight. But I'd like to know more about why you feel the way you do about the past. I expect something like that from someone Ruth's age, not a young woman." When he noticed the wary expression on Lori's face, he apologized. "Don't mind me. It so happens that I'm the director of the historical society, which means I'm constantly juggling history with current concerns. It has a way of getting in the way of many of my conversations. Can I show you anymore?"

The director? This man could turn out to be her boss after tomorrow. And she'd let him come too close tonight—emotionally as well as physically. She supposed she should tell him more about herself and why she was here, but that would turn tonight from the mystical thing it was into a business conversation. And as long as he was this close to her, she didn't have the strength to shatter the mood. "No," she said softly. Then, although the words were hard to say, she continued. "I've taken too much of your time already."

"Time is something I have a lot of at night. Come on. You're shivering. Let's see if we can find the road without getting eaten up by the vines."

Lori managed not to draw away until Shade had her back on the gravel drive, but as soon as she could take a step without subjecting her ankles to any more thorns, she freed herself from his enveloping arm. It was only the dark, the mist, their primitive surroundings, that made her want to cling to this experience. And to him. "I appreciate the tour," she managed lamely. "I feel rather foolish inconveniencing you like this." She started toward her car.

Shade stopped her. "I'm going that way myself. My car's parked on the road leading to the barn. That's something I think you'd like to see in the daylight. It's over a hundred years old."

Lori concentrated on walking, her now-numb toes unable to discern the tiny hills and valleys in the road. She listened absently as Shade told her about the barn's uses over the years, the need to replace rotted timbers, but the sound of his voice rather than the words themselves were what reached her. His voice seemed to come from a place so deep in his chest that it had to struggle to make its way out. It spoke of strength, masculinity, competence. A man she couldn't even see shouldn't have a voice like that. It made keeping her hands off him harder than it should have been.

At last Shade had her back to her car. He stepped away from her and ran his hand along the car's front fender. "What is it, an old Mustang?"

"A 1965 Mustang," Lori said proudly. She couldn't deny that it was much easier to breathe, to think, now that his attention was focused on the car. "My father bought it for me when it came time for my first car. I'll probably never sell it."

"I should hope not. They're worth more now than they ever were. They're unique cars, mavericks."

Like me, Lori thought. "It still needs a new muffler. Unfortunately, nothing lasts forever," Lori said as she tried to reach into her wet pants for the car keys. She tugged them loose. "Again, thanks. I hope you don't catch cold."

"People don't catch cold from the rain. They get that from other people. Are you sure you know your way out of here? It's a pretty isolated part of the county."

Lori saw Shade's hand reaching for her and shied away. She'd been touched enough for one night. It was too hard to keep her mind on track when he did that. "Yes. No problem," she muttered, trying to reach for the doorknob without it looking too obvious that she was avoiding contact.

Ryan pulled back his hand. "Don't be afraid of me, Lori Jordan Black. I'm not going to eat you up."

You're right, Lori admitted silently. *No man's ever going to try to do that to me again.*

Chapter Two

Lori turned on the car heater, but she'd located her motel before she stopped shivering. She paid for one night's lodging and walked out of the office before the manager could say anything about her sodden appearance. The motel complex wasn't much in the looks department, but then Lori's pocketbook didn't allow for any luxuries. If she got the job, she'd have to find low-rent housing in a hurry. Darn! She should have asked Shade more about the job she'd come here to apply for. She would have if only—if only his masculinity hadn't gotten in the way.

Forget it, she tried to tell herself. *That isn't going to happen again. The next time you see him, he could very well be your boss. There won't be room for those kinds of thoughts then.*

The interior of her motel room did nothing to raise Lori's spirits. The one picture on the wall behind the sagging double bed came straight out of a discount store. The curtain rod sagged, allowing the gray drapes to drag along the floor. There were a couple of stains in the faded orange carpet and a cigarette burn in the bedspread. But Lori had come here to get a night's sleep, not critique the place. As long as the shower was hot—

Well, warm was better than cold, Lori acknowledged after turning the faucet all the way to the left failed to produce any steam in the unheated room. She stood, still shivering slightly under the spray, her short dark hair a wet hood over her eyebrows. Lori had a fatalistic but realistic attitude toward her hair. She would have liked to let the cocoa mop grow, but her hair was so heavy that its weight dragged it down. As long as she kept it cropped just below her ears and to the base of her neck, its natural curl gave her hair enough bounce that she seldom bothered with rollers. She was still trying to get her bangs to part, but they seemed determined to flirt with her thick eyebrows. If she were a man and wanted to grow a beard, she'd wind up looking like a grizzly bear. A short, skinny man with five pounds of fuzz on his face.

Lori giggled and started to soap vigorously to try to return circulation to her chilled arms and legs. Poor Black Bob. It didn't seem fair that one of the biggest loggers to ever go into the woods should have a daughter who would blow away in a good storm. At least she was strong, Lori acknowledged, flexing her arm. All right, so she probably couldn't fight off the advances of a determined man, but at least being a size eight didn't mean she had to stand around looking helpless when a lid needed opening. She could even change the tires on her Mustang. Hadn't she packed her belongings and loaded them into her car while Brett was still trying to convince her that she was going to get herself killed without him around to run interference.

Poor Brett. All he wanted was a wife who believed in this thing called togetherness. It wasn't his fault that he'd married a woman who'd grown up hearing the wind whistling through the tops of mountain pines more often than she heard the sound of a human voice.

I hope you're happy, Brett, Lori thought as she got out of the shower. *You have to be happier without me than you were when we were together.*

And she? Was she any happier?

Lori had to admit that she was. She hadn't bothered to turn on the TV in the room, but she'd never cared much for the sound that came from a TV. Her room was quiet, almost as quiet as it had been out at the Kadin farm. Besides, although she wasn't sure she wanted to admit it, it was easier to remember the moments she'd spent with Shade Ryan with silence wrapped around her.

She liked it there, she admitted. The place was made for someone like her. Of course that was a hurdle she'd have to cross tomorrow. She didn't dare think ahead to what she wanted to do at the ranch until she knew whether the job as horticultural consultant was hers. At least her credentials were good. She was a licensed horticulturist with four years of experience out of college. Despite the divorce, Brett was willing to supply her with pictures, drawings and other proof of the work she'd done through Jordan Landscaping. She'd done two extensive garden restorations around historic buildings in the past year. If that didn't give her some experience in historical landscaping, she didn't know what would. Besides, Lori wanted the job because it would allow her to spend her days outdoors.

Lori pulled a paperback out of her overnight bag and curled up in bed. After one night here her flesh would be practically crawling with the need to be outside. That's why she'd walked around in the mist tonight; because she'd spent the day in a car.

She supposed she'd have to tell Shade Ryan that, but it wasn't the kind of emotion that equated well with words. "I don't like being inside. I'm not comfortable around people. I have to have space around me. That's why I wanted to wander around an overgrown old ranch in the middle of the night." She had a pretty good idea what Shade would think if she told him that.

Lori read until her lids refused to stay open. She slipped out of bed to make sure her door was locked and then snapped off the bedside light. Because she wasn't used to the sounds outside the motel room, she slept restlessly, but at least she was warm. The small apartment she'd moved into after she and Brett separated had a single bed. This was the first double bed she'd been in, in three months. Her fading thoughts were of her reactions to a man despite the fact that they were light-years away from sharing any kind of bed. It wasn't right. It made no sense. And yet there was no denying what she'd felt when Shade touched her—and even when he hadn't.

As Lori was getting ready the next morning, she admitted that leaving a marriage bed had been much less of an adjustment than most people would expect. In fact, the emotions she'd felt last night when Shade stood next to her in the rain came a lot closer to reaching her sexually than sleeping with her husband had.

Stop that! Lori warned herself. *I thought you settled that last night.* She raked a brush through her springy locks and pushed her bangs away long enough to add a touch of gray shadow to her eyes and stepped back. Cow eyes. That's what they were. Big and brown and soft like a cow's. A few years ago they sparkled with enthusiasm for life. The sparkle had faded just as her eyes seemed to have deepened. Her lips seemed to have forgotten how to smile, but the touch of wary vulnerability around her mouth went with watchful eyes. She didn't expect it to be any different. She wasn't a teenager thinking the world was her oyster. Lori was a woman who'd tried marriage and togetherness and come out of it admitting she wasn't designed for getting that close to a man. If her eyes revealed lonely resignation, there wasn't anything she could do about it.

Maybe that was going to change now, she thought as she pulled on a soft brushed knit sweater and smoothed it over tapered trousers. Her outfit, she hoped, struck the right balance between recommended attire for a standard job interview and the fact that she was interviewing for physical outdoor work. Lori had never worn jewelry except for her wedding ring, and the mark around the base of her finger no longer existed. The lack of glitter, hopefully, was more proof of her pragmatic approach to work.

It was time to take her portfolio and stomachful of butterflies over to the museum that housed the offices of the local historical society and present her case. Either she'd be hired as the horticulturist to do the landscaping restoration work on the historic Kadin farm, or she'd get a job in a nursery somewhere. Whatever happened, she'd make do. She always had.

THE COUNTY MUSEUM was housed in a two-story brick building surrounded by over an acre of shaded grassland. Lori guessed that the building was over a hundred years old and gave silent credit to whoever was responsible for its upkeep. Humans should age as well as this building, she admitted as she found a parking space at the rear and got out. She felt unsteady on her unaccustomed heels, but at least she wouldn't be expected to dress like this on the job—if she got it.

Lori pushed open the high, heavy, solid-wood doors and returned the receptionist's smile. When the woman tried to hand Lori a visitor's book to sign, Lori explained that she was here for a job interview. "I don't know the person's name," she admitted. "I was told to ask for whoever does the hiring."

"Of course. Why don't you go into his office." The sixtyish woman pointed toward a door across the hall from her station.

Lori gave her a shaky smile and stepped into a high-ceilinged room dominated by one of those massive machines used for viewing material stored on microfilm. Behind the machine was a young man perched on a desk, talking on the phone. He pointed Lori past him to yet another room.

This room had the same high ceiling and long narrow windows, but Lori barely noticed that. She was scarcely aware of a desk heavy enough to need support under it. It was the man getting to his feet behind the desk who commanded her attention.

"Lori Jordan Black. I was expecting you."

Ryan was surprised by how good, how new, Lori's name sounded rolling off his tongue. He'd said it to himself enough times last night and this morning that it should have felt comfortable by now. As he watched her blink in surprise, he kicked himself for not telling her last night that he was responsible for the hiring that took place in the society. But last night had been special in a way he didn't have words for. He hadn't wanted to risk the magic he'd felt in the dark by bringing in any more reality than necessary.

God, she looked fantastic! He missed the dripping

T-shirt he could barely see, but watching her walk in here in full light made up for the loss. It was insane to feel like a teenager on his first date simply because he was getting to his feet and stretching out his hand for an unnecessary but totally satisfying handshake, but it was impossible to deny what he was feeling. All meetings between men and women should take place on a misting night in the middle of what could pass for wilderness. It gave the experience a taste, a sense even, that carried over to the next day when the everyday threatened to intrude.

"Ryan, Shade Ryan. And I'm not supposed to ask you where the name came from." She stared at what little of her hand hadn't been covered by the larger one.

"You remember well," he said in a voice remarkably without emotion, considering what he was feeling. "Sit down, please. You don't look nearly as bedraggled as you did last night."

Lori sank into the stiff brocade chair Shade indicated and stared boldly at him. Late thirties, she decided. And more concerned with what was in his head than on his back. Despite her surprise at learning that he would be interviewing her, she wasn't angry. "I wish you'd told me," she said honestly, simply.

Shade sat down and leaned back in the swivel office chair. He shrugged his shoulders as if trying to adjust his sports jacket. He met her eyes without wavering. "I thought about it. But I have to wear so many hats. It was kind of nice just being a tour guide. Please don't hold it against me. After all, I did introduce myself. I just didn't add that I'm also the personnel officer here."

Another two seconds of locking eyes with Shade and Lori knew she would never hold Shade's silence against him. She'd been right about one thing last night: he was certainly attractive. His hair was thick, somewhere between blond and gray with an interesting mix of curls that seemed to have only a casual relationship with each other. Bushy eyebrows served as a gate to green eyes set deep in prominent cheekbones. Lori's eyes slid to his large nose, his square jaw. This wasn't what the director of a historical society was supposed to look like.

Lori took a deep breath to settle her butterflies and tried on a shaky smile. "Have you read my résumé? I've done work on several historic places."

"I know. But those were homes, not farms. We're looking for a different treatment at the Kadin farm. Do you understand what the society has in mind?"

"I think so," Lori admitted, grateful that the conversation had turned to business. "In the letter that accompanied the pictures of the farm, you, or whoever wrote the letter, said that the Kadin place was being turned over to the historical society for restoration and display purposes."

"That's the bare bones of the concept," Shade said, his smile coming easily. "Don't mind me. I'm kind of excited about the project, much more than I am about, say, a display of pioneer-era dolls. There aren't any old-style farms left, and that's a shame. People want to know what it was like to live off the land a hundred or more years ago. The Kadin farm is going to give us the opportunity to show people that. Our plans are to take things back a hundred years, run chickens in the front yard, raise vegetables up to the door, bring in both beef and dairy cattle, set up butter churns, reestablish the root cellar, put on display all those things grandparents love to talk to their grandchildren about. But first—"

Shade folded his considerable arms across his even more considerable chest. "First we have to cut a path through the underbrush so people don't get lost in there. That's where you come in."

You? Lori wondered if he was saying the job was hers but knew enough not to assume too much. "I wish I'd seen the place in the light," she admitted. "I only have a vague idea of what needs doing."

"But you do agree that the jungle has to be tamed?"

Lori thought about the scrape marks still on her ankles. "I'm afraid so. I'm not sure, but I think those were blackberries I ran into. They'll take over everything if they're not stopped."

"They already have. Blackberries and several kinds of vines and ivy. I'm not an expert in that department, but I know there's a lot of mistletoe in the trees, and some of the trees are badly decayed. It's a shame, because some of the oaks are hundreds of years old. What I'm trying to say is, nothing's been done to the garden for over twenty years. That has to be done, but at the same time I don't want it to look as if we came in and clear-cut. The Kadin family spent three generations working on the landscaping. We have to remain faithful to that."

"I understand. You don't want a historic farmhouse smack in the middle of something that looks like a city park. You want a natural surrounding for those chickens and dairy cows."

"You do understand." Shade got to his feet and again stuck out his hand. "Welcome aboard, Lori Jordan Black."

"I have the job?"

Shade smiled. "You have the job. When can you start?"

Lori felt slightly weak, but at least her butterflies were departing. She had a job! She was launched! "Please call me Lori Black. That's the name I'll be going by."

"I'm glad to meet you, Lori Black, for the second time. Now, unless you're in a hurry, I'd like to introduce you to some of the staff members."

Lori surrendered herself to Shade for the next hour, scrambling after him as he took her to the far recesses of the massive old building. She met a man who did nothing but catalog artifacts and a dynamite woman who was directing a play on the history of suffrage that would be going into every school and community theater in the county. She watched in amazement as a seamstress took tiny tucks in a handmade wedding gown and then poked her way through the most complete darkroom she'd ever seen, which existed for the sole purpose of recording history.

"I had no idea there was this much to a historical society," Lori admitted when, somehow, Shade had brought her back to his office.

"You ain't seen nothing yet. Wait until you see the historical library. With all the interest in family histories, the material there is always in use. What did you expect, little old ladies dusting off moldy books?"

"Something like that," Lori admitted. "But I shouldn't have. After all, you don't look anything like a historical society director."

"Why? Because I don't wear metal-frame glasses perched on the end of my nose? I know. I look like a wrestling coach. Sorry to disappoint you."

Lori sidestepped his comment by asking Shade when he wanted her to report for work. He explained that Monday would be soon enough and then asked her for a phone number where she could be reached.

"I don't have one right now," Lori admitted. "I'm staying at a motel."

"You're new to the area?" He sounded concerned.

"I'm new to the state. I've just come from California."

"Where you were Lori Jordan. Don't worry," he reassured her. "I'm not going to ask. There's something in the regulations that says an employer doesn't have the right to ask an employee personal questions. But now that I know you're living in a motel, can I give you a piece of advice?"

Lori nodded. At least they were back in his office with the door closed where no one else could hear their conversation. She just didn't want her newly divorced status to go beyond these walls until she'd had a chance to get to know the people she'd be working with. She already felt as if she knew Shade.

"Good. Try to find a house, not an apartment," Shade was saying. "I can't recommend any of those complexes you'll find in the classified section."

"I'd never live in an apartment," Lori said quickly, and then dropped her eyes to cover up anything they might reveal. "I mean—" she started again. "There's nothing wrong with an apartment. They're just not right for me."

"Maybe—" Shade paused. For a moment his green eyes turned almost black. "Damn, I keep telling myself I'm going to turn over a new leaf, stop trying to run other people's lives. But maybe this isn't butting in. Maybe it's helping out a couple of people. I have a friend. Actually, I have an ex-wife who got our house in the divorce settlement but has departed with a friend to tour Europe before deciding what she wants to do with the rest of her life. The house is just sitting there housing spiders and asking to be broken into. How would you like to stay there?"

As quickly as the butterflies had left, they returned. This time they were in full flight for another reason, a reason surely Shade couldn't understand. "Why don't you stay there?" Lori blurted out while trying to find the words to turn him down.

"Because I have my own place now. And because I'm not crazy about going back to the memories. Look." Shade rested his elbows on the table, bringing him closer to Lori. He'd had no intention of telling her that much about his emotions and didn't understand why the words had come out. Even his ex-wife didn't know why he'd been so quick to turn the house over to her. "Why don't you think about it," he said quickly, because it was too late to take back what he'd begun. "I can take you to the place, show you around. If you like solitude and elbow room, you'll like it."

Lori pasted on a smile and forced herself to use a light tone. "Are you sure you trust me? After all, you hardly know me."

"I know more about you than you think I do, Lori. I know that the work at the farm is going to be more than just a paycheck to you. I know you'd like to reach out and touch people but something's holding you back." Those words came easily.

Lori sucked in her breath and dropped her eyes. Shade, her employer, wasn't supposed to say something as personal as that. Besides, he was wrong. She was comfortable with her solitude. "I don't think it's such a good idea—about the house, I mean," she stammered. "I mean, you're my boss."

"I'm also the guy who kept you from getting swallowed up in a jungle last night. Don't say no until you've seen the house." In the space of a few seconds Shade's emotions had taken a complete turnaround. He was now sure of what he was doing. He wanted Lori Black in the empty house. "I think you're going to change your mind." Shade rose to his feet and came around to her side of the desk. Before Lori could prepare herself, he offered his hand to help her out of her chair. He stood near, very near, his hand on her shoulder. "Why don't you come back here at five. I'll show you the house."

"I don't want to inconvenience you. Really, I can find a place of my own."

"I don't think so." Shade still had his hand around her shoulder. "Go ahead, look. And if you haven't found something by five, we'll talk." He pulled her closer, forcing her off balance and onto her toes as he brought her a hairbreadth away from his hard, athletic body. She could feel his warm breath disturbing her always-unruly bangs. "I don't think I'm reading you wrong, Lori. I think you're going to fall in love with the place."

Lori waited, not breathing, until Shade released her. He'd already turned to a blinking light on his telephone, but it was a few more seconds before Lori was able to pull her eyes from him and grope for the door.

Why had he touched her like that, she asked as she was getting back into her Mustang. This wasn't the way a man like Shade Ryan should be acting just after he'd hired a young, single female employee. He had no right. Just because she was divorced didn't mean she was fair game.

Lori joined the traffic on the street that went past the museum and tried to concentrate on the message her empty stomach was trying to get across. Oh, yes, she knew all about what men thought of divorced women. She hadn't been divorced long enough to have experienced it firsthand more than once or twice, but she wasn't naive enough to think she'd be able to fade into the woodwork once a man learned she no longer wore a wedding ring, no longer had someone to reach for in bed.

Well, Shade Ryan was going to be sadly disappointed. What the man didn't know was that lovemaking had never been a crucial part of her marriage. Lori had enjoyed making love on occasion, but the rockets she'd heard about were only so much hype. Surrendering her body to Brett had done more to make her pull away from, than to enhance their relationship. Brett wanted them to share everything—work, thoughts, feelings, emotions, the most intimate experiences. Unfortunately, he'd chosen a wife who was incapable of blending her being with him. Brett wanted them to live as one; Lori had been raised to rely on herself and no one else. Just because Shade Ryan was very, very handsome—she wouldn't deny that—didn't mean Lori could forget what she'd learned from her marriage.

She was a private person. Her personality didn't allow for the kind of relationship men wanted. What Shade had to understand was that sharing a mystical experience last night didn't mean she was about to forget who and what she was. She'd have to tell him that—somehow.

Lori grabbed a quick breakfast at a drive-up window and then bought a local newspaper. Between getting lost a half-dozen times and staring at the map until her eyes blurred, to say nothing of having to look at a cookie-cutter assortment of apartments without yards, she was soon sorry she'd wolfed down her meal. The few houses listed were either in undesirable neighborhoods or priced way beyond her budget.

Weren't there any decent rentals available anywhere in the city, Lori wondered. Brett had wanted them to live in a modern apartment complex with swimming pool, sauna and tennis court. The one thing Lori had learned from that experience was that she'd rather pitch a tent next to the railroad tracks than live where she had to keep her drapes closed to prevent her neighbors from looking in the bedroom window.

Despite herself, Lori's thoughts returned to what her boss had said. Shade was sure she'd fall in love with the house. Even mild interest would be a giant leap from what she was feeling about the cheaply constructed cracker boxes she'd be able to afford. As she drove past yet another house, situated so close to its neighbors that it didn't have a strip of grass on the side, Lori couldn't help but focus on what Shade had said about elbow room.

You're spoiled. That's what's wrong, Lori chided herself. Black Bob had never been able to provide his daughter with fancy housing, but the cabins they'd lived in while he followed the timber industry around the northwest had vistas that would put any penthouse to shame. How anyone could settle for a view of another high rise when they'd grown up surrounded by mountains covered with evergreens and free running rivers was something she was afraid she'd never be able to do.

It was as simple as that. Lori had grown up in the woods. That had ruined her for city life.

Lori settled on an ice cream cone for lunch to counteract the heat inside her car and went back to running down rentals. As five o'clock neared, she admitted she was dismissing possible rentals without giving them a chance.

Out of desperation she wound up back at the museum near tears and trying to resign herself to another night in a motel room. It hadn't been hard to find a place to stay when she left Brett, but then she'd fallen into a stroke of luck—a historic old barn of a house that was going to undergo restoration in a few months and was sitting empty for the time being.

She wouldn't blame Shade for laughing if she admitted defeat. Maybe she should just crawl back to the motel and redouble her efforts tomorrow.

No. Tomorrow wouldn't change what she'd learned today.

She spotted Shade coming out a side door, his arm draped over a middle-aged woman as he leaned toward her, listening intently. At the last moment Lori's courage almost failed her. She wasn't going to admit defeat to him. She wasn't going to risk having a man she was physically attracted to stretch out a helping hand. But before she could climb back into her Mustang, Shade spotted her and said his good-byes to the gray-haired woman.

"Don't tell me," he said as he approached. "It was even worse than you thought it would be."

"How did you know?" she asked, too tired to argue.

"Have you looked at yourself lately? You were wearing lipstick this morning. That's gone. Your hair has lost its bounce, your slacks are wrinkled, and unless I miss my guess, you traded your heels for tennis shoes."

"Oh," Lori stammered. "Do I really look that bad?"

"You look like you'd like to cry. Did anyone ever tell you that your eyes give away everything? They're telling me that you're getting ready to wave that white flag of surrender.''

"Oh," Lori said again, and blinked, wondering if the gesture could wipe away what her eyes were revealing. "It's just that I kept getting turned around and it was hot and—"

"Don't try to explain." Shade draped a surprisingly heavy arm over her shoulder. "I knew it was going to be like that. Well, what do you want to do first? Eat or see the house?"

"I don't expect you to feed me," Lori said quickly, wondering how she was going to wriggle out from under his arm without calling attention to the fact that she didn't feel at all calm having him touching her.

"And I don't want you passing out on me. You look damn close to that point about now. Look, do you think you could indulge me? Kind of a trade-off for my feeding you."

"What are you talking about?" She had no idea how she was going to say no to a man whose arm felt as if it were touching places deep inside her.

Shade's eyes left her face and strayed to the Mustang. "Let me drive your car. I've never driven one of those old classics." He winked. "I'd consider it ample payment for your dinner."

Lori tried to protest, but Shade didn't give her time. He was steering her toward the passenger side as if an argument were the last thing he expected.

In the end Lori relented, not because she thought his proposal was a fair exchange but because her day had left her without the energy to talk, let alone argue. *I know how to be an employee,* she told herself. *It isn't that hard to do.*

She tried to concentrate on the traffic and Shade's

ability to handle the loose steering, but the car's rocking motion and the breeze coming in the open window were her undoing. Her lids closed, and she surrendered to her head's need to rest against the back of the seat. She was dozing off, lulled by the all-music station Shade had tuned to. After dinner she'd tell him that she'd consider staying in his house only under the circumstances that there were no strings attached. After dinner—

"I hate to disturb you, but we're here."

Lori fought through the fog and forced her eyes to focus. They'd left the valley floor and were now in the low hills surrounding the city. The road they were on was narrow and winding, but because hers was the only car on the road it seemed ample enough.

"I wanted you to see what it looks like around here before we get to the house," Shade was explaining. He went on to tell her that the area was outside the city limits but the county maintained the road and the homes used city water. "It's just high enough off the valley floor to be another world. There's a two-acre-minimum lot size for all houses on the side of the hill. It makes for slightly higher taxes, but I thought it was worth it."

Lori turned. There was that softly sad note to Shade's voice again. Obviously the house had meant something to him. "Did you have the house built for you?" Lori asked in an effort to understand more.

Shade shook his head. "I'd like to do that someday, but right now a house is simply a place for me to hang my hat. I don't know if Vicky is going to hold on to this place. That's her decision."

Lori didn't speak again until Shade had pulled off the winding road and eased the car down a short gravel drive. They were at the back side of the house, which gave her little more than a view of the garage and a feeling of space. Pine trees, which were probably the only plantings that could get a foothold in the steep terrain, grew all around the house. "The developers didn't cut any of the trees," she observed.

"That's part of what I fell in love with. That and the view."

Lori got out and joined Shade as he unlocked the front door. They stepped inside, and he turned on a light. The entryway opened into a massive living room with a high beamed ceiling, rock fireplace and a massive sliding-glass door at the far end. Lori was drawn to the door.

She gasped. "It's unreal!" The thick double glass door opened on to a large raised redwood deck that jutted out over the side of the hill. Below and on both sides was a true mountain of evergreens. Far below she could make out the valley, a layer of smog blurring the image of road and houses. "Oh, Shade!" She turned toward him. "This is what I grew up surrounded by. How could you ever leave this?"

"I didn't have much choice." Shade continued to look at the view and not her. "Do you want to see the rest of the house?"

Chastised, Lori trailed after him. She'd been so insensitive. Shade made it clear that his wife had gotten the house in the divorce settlement. She should have thought before she asked him why he'd left it. She didn't believe a word he said about a house simply being a place to hang one's hat. This home was a refuge, sanity.

Five minutes later they were back in the oversized, thick-carpeted living room. The house had three bedrooms, a cozy family room with built-in bookshelves and a modern kitchen complete with island preparation area. What struck Lori the most was that there weren't any drapes in the house. That, she hoped, would be a safe topic.

"That's what I've always pictured for my dream home," she admitted. "I can't think of anything nicer than not having to have curtains." She didn't add that the house was telling her a great deal about the man who had just become her boss.

"That's what I thought," Shade said as he settled his frame in a couch facing the decking. "But Vicky says that's the worst part about staying here alone. She doesn't feel she has any privacy."

"Oh, no," Lori blurted out. "There's all the privacy in the world here. There's nothing but trees all around. I don't even see lights from the neighbors' houses. I can't think of anything more perfect."

Shade sighed. "I guess it takes all kinds. Anyway, that's going to be a problem, deciding what to do with the place. What do you think? Think you'd like to stay here until Vicky makes up her mind?"

Lori chewed on her lower lip and pretended to be studying the view. There was no denying it; the house was perfect. But it belonged to another woman. If she stayed here, it would link her to Shade in a way she wasn't sure she could handle. It wasn't just exhaustion that made her sense there could be more to their relationship than what existed now. "It's beautiful," she managed. "But I can't afford it."

"You don't have to. That's not part of the deal. I just want someone staying here."

"Shade, I can't."

Lori had been standing with her back to Shade, her

eyes trained on the unbelievable panorama of solid evergreens just beyond the high deck. She sensed that he was getting to his feet, but she didn't expect him to put his arm on her shoulders and pull her toward him.

"Why?" he whispered against the back of her neck.

Because I'm not sure I can handle the effect you're having on me. "Because your—Vicky might come back. She doesn't want to find me staying here."

"Vicky will be gone for six weeks."

Oh. A stupid statement on her part. It might have to do with his breath disturbing her neckline hairs. Or it might be the feel of his hard chest pressing against her back. "I don't know what to say. It's beautiful." And what her soul needed, she admitted.

"Then say yes."

"Yes."

She sensed as well as heard Shade's sigh. "That was easy," he whispered.

"No, it wasn't," she admitted. "Shade? I don't know how to say this." She stopped a moment, grateful that she didn't have to look into his eyes and yet knowing that physical contact was just as hard to counteract. "You—you're my boss. I don't know if it's wise for you to be my landlord, as well."

Shade turned her around. He looked down into the eyes of the woman looking up at him. He'd been dreading having to come back into the house, but even with a thousand memories crowding around him, it was easier than he thought it would be. The reason, he knew, was because there was someone else in the house with him.

No. Not just someone else. A woman who had already become more important to him than he thought possible.

"I don't know if it's wise, either," he admitted. "But you want to be here. I can sense it. I want you here."

"Thank you," he heard her whisper. When she said nothing more, he realized that the mood enveloping him was touching her, as well. If he didn't stay absolutely still, didn't clamp his lips together, he would be leaning over and kissing her. And once his lips had tasted hers, he wasn't sure that would be enough. He felt it in his loins; given any kind of encouragement, he would spend the night with this woman.

Chapter Three

A half hour later Shade and Lori were at a casual, dimly lit Chinese restaurant, sipping tea while waiting for their meals. Lori had tried to beg off because she'd sensed something dangerous in her reaction to Shade before he finally let her go, but before she could react to that something, his mood suddenly changed. With a boyish grin Shade informed her that he was close to starving, and besides, she'd better eat before unloading her full trunk and back seat.

"You look a bit like a gypsy driving round with boxes in the back seat," Shade observed. He'd removed his sport coat and undone the top two buttons on his dress shirt. It made him look, Lori thought, like a man who knew how to make the most of the hours after 5:00 P.M.

"I suppose I do," Lori admitted. "But it's all I own in the world, so it really isn't that much."

Shade gave a mock groan. "Where did I go wrong? I turned over the house and agreed to support Vicky for a year until she found herself. I should have had your huband's attorney."

"I didn't ask for anything," Lori admitted, and then drew a curtain over the past. She turned the conversation around by asking Shade how he'd become director of a historical society. "You really don't look the part," she pointed out. She couldn't help looking at his mop of hair. Unless he was going through a delayed adolescence, he was long overdue for a haircut.

As if reading her thoughts, Shade raked large fingers through his hair. "I keep forgetting to go to the barber. It's a good thing I'm qualified for the job, because you're probably right. I've always suspected that I don't fit the image. If you promise you won't fall asleep, I'll tell you the whole story. I was raised in San Francisco by parents who were passionately committed to just about any restoration or preservation cause they heard about. Maybe it's part of San Francisco, a reverence for the past, I don't know. I rather suspect the cable cars have something to do with it. Anyway, I guess there was no escaping it. I was bitten by the same bug that infected my parents. When I wasn't pumping iron, I was reading history books and tromping through museums. Other kids my age thought I was rather strange."

"You pumped iron?" A little of Lori's tea slopped over as she put down her tiny cup. She'd been able to dismiss his maleness for a couple of minutes, but its impact returned with his words.

"That isn't what a historical society director is supposed to do?" Shade's grin was positively juvenile. "What you have to realize is that when I was in college, I didn't know what I wanted to do with my life. Like most kids, I'd given up on being a fireman but couldn't think of a practical alternative. Physical fitness was what I did when I didn't want to think. I was toying with becoming a lawyer, but my father died during my senior year. It was time to get out in the world and earn my keep."

Lori didn't say anything. It was obvious that Shade's

father's death had affected him profoundly. She wanted to say she understood, but she'd only been a baby when her mother died. She'd never felt the need to mourn someone she didn't know.

"I guess I got where I am the way most people do," Shade wound up. "The right situation comes around at the right time. At least it was right for me. I enjoy what I do."

"I'm glad," Lori said softly as their egg flower soup was delivered.

"What about you?" Shade pressed. "I've been boring you with my life story. How did a little thing like you get to be a horticulturist?"

For some reason Lori didn't take offense to being called a little thing. Shade had just hired her because of her brains and experience. The expression was probably simply an attempt to keep the conversation light. She met Shade's green eyes. "I was raised in the mountains. My father is a lumberjack, but he has a great reverence and respect for the land. I got that from him. I've always loved working with living things." Lori paused and then decided to fill in the blanks. "My mother was killed when I was two. Her car was hit by a truck."

Shade reached out his hand and covered Lori's. "I'm sorry."

"Don't be," Lori said simply. His touch was all she needed to continue. "I never knew her. My father did a remarkable job of raising a daughter alone. Every time we had to move to a new job, he'd plop me in the truck next to him, and we'd be off. Black Bob was my best friend as well as being my father."

"I'm glad to hear that," Shade said as he went back to his soup. "But it must have been a rather lonely upbringing if your father didn't put down any roots. Didn't you miss having friends, other family around?"

"How can you miss something you've never experienced?" Lori didn't usually say much about her private thoughts. Maybe it was the combination of a long, exhausting day and warm soup filling her empty stomach. Maybe it was green eyes and unruly hair. "Not every human is a social creature. Some of us prefer our own company."

"A loner, huh. Is that what you're telling me you are?"

"I guess I am."

"Don't be so sure, Lori," Shade said, locking eyes with her again. "We all need someone." He wanted to tell her that he was speaking from experience, but there was nothing that said they shared the same emotions. All he knew for sure was that he'd only known her for twenty-four hours and yet already he didn't like the thought of her being alone. It wasn't that he resented her independence. In fact, he found that a fascinating aspect of who she was. But he couldn't shake the fact that she hadn't tried to pull out of his arms when they were in the house earlier. He could simply be reading what he wanted to into her reaction, but he didn't think so. No matter what Lori might think, she needed that human contact.

The conversation switched to safer topics during dinner. When they were getting ready to leave, Shade informed her that he was going to follow her back to the house in his car to help her unpack. He didn't care what she thought of his protective gesture. He wouldn't feel right leaving her alone like that. But, he admitted, he wouldn't stay long. He wanted to, and that wasn't safe for their newborn relationship.

"It isn't necessary," Lori protested, suddenly embarrassed by her meager belongings. "I loaded the car. I can unload it."

"You're going to turn down a weight lifter? If you don't put me to work, I'll just have to go to the gym for an hour to get some exercise."

Lori had no argument to work around that kind of logic. It was, after all, his house. Besides, as Shade pointed out after they'd driven to where his car was parked, there were some things about the house he needed to show her. Lori let Shade lead the way, slightly embarrassed because she'd been dozing and not paying attention the first time they went into the hills.

It was dark when they reached the house, but Shade deposited her safely inside. He switched on several outside lights, and almost before she could lend a hand, had her pile of belongings stacked in the living room.

"What's in there?" he asked. "Clothes. What else?"

Lori's chin jutted out. She had nothing to be ashamed of just because his ex-wife had a grand house and she had an old Mustang filled with boxes. "Books. Everyone collects something. I collect books."

"I just hope there's a pair of garden gloves in there somewhere. You're going to need them when you show up for work Monday. This job's going to call for your brawn as well as your brains."

Lori followed Shade obediently through the house as he pointed out locks on the windows, the electrical panel in the garage, the workings of the outside lighting system. "Standard model," he wound up. "The number for the fire department and police is by the phone. Well, do you think you can handle things here?"

Lori nodded, feeling dismissed. For some strange

reason she wasn't in a hurry to have him leave, but apparently Shade had more to do with his evening than spend it here. She noted that he was watching her every move, but because that made her uncomfortable, she concentrated on the duties expected of a hostess. She walked with him toward the door, wondering why he no longer walked with his usual spring. "I'll see you Monday morning, then," she said when she wondered if he was going to continue to stand in the doorway looking at her until she felt as if she had to hide from him. "Do you want me to come to the museum or go right out to the farm?"

"The farm. I'll be there at eight." Shade opened the door, stepped out and then turned back toward her. "You're sure you feel comfortable here?" He was silhouetted against the night, a voice without form. Unfortunately for the sake of Lori's sanity, her senses were filling in the shadows.

"I told you. I'm a loner."

"I know. I just—never mind. You don't want me hovering over you, do you? I understand. Or at least I'm trying to."

Lori closed the door behind Shade and turned back toward the living room. Most of her mind stayed with Shade, making the journey down the hill with him. It was so quiet that she could hear the sound of crickets outside. Shade's tires crunched along the gravel drive and faded away.

Alone.

Lori picked up a suitcase and carried it into the master bedroom. She still felt a little like Cinderella let loose in the palace, but the impact of her surroundings took second place to other emotions.

It was a strange thing about being alone, Lori

thought as she rummaged through her belongings for a nightgown. She hadn't minded the long hours in a car on her way here from California. She'd used the time to think about her marriage and all the reasons why it had gone wrong. She hadn't found any answers, but she hadn't fought the search, either.

Lori pulled her sweater over her head and let wrinkled pants slide off her slim legs. Her bra took a quick flip of the wrist; a moment later she was naked. The nightgown was slightly crumpled, but it smoothed out as she pulled the gathered bodice, spaghetti straps and long skirt over her body. Her breasts filled the bodice and gave definition to the soft fabric. She shook her head briefly in an effort to rearrange her hair and then padded barefoot into the living room.

Lori checked the front door to make sure she'd locked it and then stood for at least five minutes on the deck overlooking her domain. Tonight she wasn't thinking about the past, or the future, either. A certain presence seemed to have filled the house and gave it life. She could imagine Shade standing where she stood now, his mind filled with private thoughts as he looked down into the wilderness. She wondered if he shied away from contact with this place because of the memories it held for him or because too many unfulfilled dreams remained to haunt him.

Don't be afraid, she whispered, sending a silent message down the hill after him. *Face those dreams. Turn them into reality.*

She had no idea what that reality might be.

Despite the things she wished she had the courage to talk to Shade about, Lori slept like the dead, reluctantly pulling herself out of bed at the scandalous hour of 9:00 A.M. As she showered, she told herself that she was entitled to one morning of indulgence. She had three days before having to report to work. The only thing she had to accomplish in that time span was to unpack, buy some groceries and let Brett know where she was.

The first two items were accomplished easily. The third wasn't faced until after she'd had dinner. Lori stalled by washing her dishes instead of putting them in the dishwasher and then wandering around chasing spiderwebs and dusting. Finally, there was no ignoring the fact that Brett would be home this time of evening and probably furious at her because she hadn't so much as dropped him a note since deciding to apply for a job with the historical society.

She placed the long-distance call, picturing the third-story apartment building she hated and Brett was so proud of. His hello came before she expected it.

"It's me," Lori stated. "I'm here, and I have the job. I thought you should know."

"You really did it, didn't you? You won't be coming back."

"No, Brett. We're divorced," she declared succinctly.

"I know we're divorced." She could picture his lips closing over his perfect teeth. "I was talking about your job. You won't be coming back to Jordan Landscaping."

"No. You can hire a permanent replacement."

"I still don't understand it," Brett was saying. "We worked our tails off getting the business off the ground. It was a success. You can't deny that. All our clients commented on the fact that it was a husband-wife business."

"That was your doing, Brett," Lori pointed out. "I wanted to work on my own, remember?"

"And if you remember, I didn't want you killing yourself knocking on doors when I could offer you job security. You always were stubborn. You insisted on doing things your way."

Lori sighed. Her way. When Brett was feeling particularly hospitable, he gave her that much credit. The rest of the time he pounded away at her to let him make the business decisions, trying to convince her that he knew best.

"Aren't you going to ask me about my job?" Lori asked.

"Will you tell me about it?"

Lori bit her tongue. She couldn't blame Brett for asking that. "There isn't much I can tell you," she admitted. "I haven't started work yet. How have you been doing? Is the new woman going to work out?"

"The new woman is working out just fine, Lori. In fact, she's here right now."

If Lori expected a stab of jealousy, it didn't come. Instead, she admitted she was happy for Brett. He deserved a woman to share his life with. "I'm glad. I hope she lets you get closer to her than I did. You always wanted more than I could give."

"It didn't have to be like that. If only you'd tried harder."

Instead of wasting time trying to tell him that relationships were a two-way street, Lori gave him her phone number and asked him to give it to her father when Black Bob got in touch. "Who knows where he is now," she said. "My last letter came back marked unforwardable."

"That's what's going to happen between us some-day, Lori. I'll lose touch with you."

"Maybe," she said before hanging up. "I have no idea what's going to happen to me now."

AT ALMOST THE MOMENT Lori hung up the phone on her ex-husband, Shade was closing the door to his rented house. It wasn't the first time he'd found an excuse, any excuse, to get out of the place, but today he was fighting a silent war with himself. If he gave in to his impulses, he would get in his car and drive up the hill to where Lori was. He could tell her that he wanted to make sure the hot-water heater was working properly. He could make sure she knew the address so she could have her mail delivered there. He could—

He wasn't kidding himself. The only real reason he would have for going to the house was to listen to what her voice sounded like, to watch the way her fingers slipped through her thick hair when she tried to push her bangs aside. As Shade got into his car and stared at the keys in his hand, he asked himself an honest question. It could be that his desire to see her went no further than a sexual attraction. It certainly wouldn't be the first time he'd felt that way about a woman. Sex was one of the main reasons he'd stayed married for as long as he had.

And yet, despite the internal heat he didn't try to deny, he was also honest enough to admit that he wanted much, much more from Lori Black than a night together. *Tell me what you want out of life,* he asked the image he carried in his mind. *Let me know what makes you cry, laugh. And—listen when I tell you some things about myself.*

With a groan that revealed the weight of his decision,

Shade turned his car in the direction of a bachelor friend's house. He wanted too much from Lori Black in too short a period of time. Not only was she a private person, but she was still working her way through a ruined relationship. He had no idea whether she wanted to answer his questions or hear what he carried inside himself. That kind of honesty, if it ever came, would take time.

LORI WAS READY for Monday morning. She threw back the covers a half hour before her alarm was set to go off and pampered herself with a long shower. She dressed in a practical cotton shirt and jeans and slipped on well-worn tennis shoes. Her Mustang took a good two minutes to start. There was no getting around it. Her first paycheck was going to have to go toward getting some mechanical work done. "Hang in there, old boy," she promised the car. "I have to work for the money first."

It wasn't quite eight by the time Lori came down off the mountain, crossed the valley and traveled along the country road leading to the Kadin farm, but Shade's car was already there. She pulled in behind his Camaro in the large drive in front of the house and got out.

The place looked different by day. It still gave the impression of being a transplanted jungle, but by now it was possbile to make out the myriad species of plant life and a couple of outbuildings she hadn't seen in the dark in addition to the barn and springhouse.

She was getting ready to knock on the front door of the massive white farmhouse when she heard a whistle behind her. Shade was beckoning her from something that vaguely resembled a rose garden. It was then that she admitted Shade Ryan had never left the corners of her mind during the past three days. She walked slowly toward him, her heart feeling too much as if she'd been running. She closed her eyes briefly, trying to tell herself that she couldn't possibly be reacting the way she was.

"Ruth's just getting ready for the day," he said when she joined him. His eyes never left hers, which made it difficult for her to concentrate on what he was saying. She wondered if her eyes were giving away too much of what was going on inside. "She doesn't like company until she has her teeth in," she heard him say.

"Is it all right for us to be here? I mean, shouldn't we announce ourselves or something?" she asked so she wouldn't have time to think about what her body was telling her about being near him again.

"Oh, Ruth knows we're about," Shade said, grinning. He was standing less than a foot away, the fact that he wasn't touching her not nearly as comforting as it should have been. "There isn't much that gets past her. But she's used to my prowling around, and she won't mind if I have company. Don't forget. She's given the land to the historical society. All she asks is that she live the rest of her life here. Well, are you ready to go to work?"

Lori glanced down at her hands. It was easier to look at them than the eyes that reached deep into her own. "I don't have my gloves. But that's kind of premature. I need to take inventory of what's here first."

"That makes sense. Do you want the grand tour?" Shade grinned again. "I prefer it the way we did things the other night, but this will probably accomplish more." He inclined his head, indicating she was to follow him, and started picking his way through the neglected rosebushes. Lori divided her attention between looking for aphids in the roses and taking in Shade's attire. The sport jersey, open at the throat, gave his considerable neck the freedom it needed; the elasticized waistband of his twill pants were made for movement.

It reminded her of what he'd said about pumping iron. From the looks of him he'd kept up his exercise regimen without crossing the line and becoming one of those overmuscled jocks who grace the covers of body-building magazines. His strength was quiet, controlled, and yet something she couldn't—and didn't want to—ignore.

Shade was explaining that Ruth's mother had planted the rose garden, and Ruth was insistent that not a single bush be removed. "She's probably going to hang over your shoulder and begrudge every sucker you have to snip off. It's one of the few links she has with her mother," he said in a soft tone that told her what he knew of human emotions. "Don't let Ruth throw you. She loves this place. It bothers her that she doesn't have the energy to take care of it anymore."

Shade and Lori spent the next hour touring the five acres that surrounded the farm, nestled in the middle of seemingly endless wheat fields. Because they were sharing their morning and because the topic was one that had long fascinated her, Lori was able to concentrate on what Shade had to say and not simply on deep masculine tones.

Lori was captivated by what she was discovering and felt no hesitancy about telling Shade how she felt. Yes, blackberries had been allowed to take hold, and an unbelievable amount of pruning, trimming and major cutting back would need to be done to free the choked ground. The oaks, pines and walnut trees supported climbing vines that reached into the branches and covered many of the holes made by woodpeckers. Lori could see why the historical society people were excited about the prospect of turning the farm into a hands-on experience for people and told Shade that the same sense of excitement was filling her.

The farm's history, Shade explained, went back over 150 years, as evidenced by trees that towered over the farmhouse and reached the barn's roofline. Lori was delighted to find a greenhouse so packed with orchids that there was literally no room for one more. That was a more modern touch than the rose garden and evidence of Ruth's love for growing things. Lori was intrigued by a huge white tower with vines climbing nearly to the top and kept weathered boards in place.

Lori knew she was showing off a little when she explained to Shade that the farm setting was in a style known as gardenesque, but she had an almost juvenile desire to prove herself to him. Instead of laying out flower beds, shrubs and combinations of trees and shrubs in rigidly symmetrical patterns, as had been done since ancient times and carried over to the American colonies, gardenesque paved the way for home owners to express their individuality.

"I'm not sure the Kadin family was influenced by Andrew Jackson Downing, who stressed the approach road, or not, but there are signs of that," Lori pointed out when she realized she had Shade's full attention. "Downing's book, which was written in 1841, made the point that roads should meander so the grounds could be fully appreciated. That's the case here, with the road going near the tower and then through those oak trees."

"You've read books that go back to 1841?" Shade asked with a respect that told Lori she hadn't wasted her breath. "Was that part of the college requirement?"

"Partly," Lori explained in a lighter tone than the one she used a breath ago. "And partly because as I became more and more interested in historical restorations, I wanted to learn what influenced older garden styles. It's really fascinating when you get into it."

Shade grinned and gave her a paternal pat on the shoulder. "I'll take your word for it. I have enough to do keeping up on the research I have to do on museum artifacts. Sounds like my instincts were right. I hired the right person for the job."

"Instinct? Is that why you hired me, because you were influenced by instinct?" Lori couldn't believe Shade was serious.

"Why not?" For the first time since they'd started on their walk, Shade locked eyes with Lori. "Women aren't the only creatures with instinct. I'm a people person," he said simply. "By that I mean I enjoy people, interacting with them, finding out what makes them tick. I probably should have majored in psychology. It didn't take long for me to decide you were the right person to do the work here."

"What did you base your decision on?" Lori had to ask, because she wasn't sure she was ready to hear more about what he meant by interacting.

"I made up my mind when I saw you show up here on a rainy night."

"Oh? I'm sorry," Lori apologized, wondering if he knew how much of his strength was in his eyes. "I—it's just that I'm curious. I haven't had much experience in applying for jobs."

"Ah, Lori." Shade touched her lightly on the forearm, but his eye contact went much deeper. "I wasn't thinking about dedication nearly as much as I was thinking that I wanted to learn more about a woman who would stand out in the rain soaking wet and cold. I don't think one woman in a thousand would forsake a nice warm car for that. You came alone. You didn't have some man around as a bodyguard. Finally, you trusted me enough to wander around in a dark jungle with me. How did you know I wasn't some demented rapist?"

"I didn't think about that," Lori admitted. What she had been thinking was something she wasn't about to tell him.

"See." Shade nodded. "That's what intrigues me. You're here all alone. Yet you trusted a total stranger."

Lori drew away from the physical contact. Whatever Shade was doing, he was moving too fast for her. "I'll have to be careful about doing that again. I have a bad habit of getting wrapped up in what I'm doing. I don't think about myself very much."

"You should." His voice dropped to a whisper again. "You're very interesting. I find you fascinating."

"I think you should be more interested in my qualifications than the fact that I'm crazy enough to wander around in the middle of the night. Don't you think we should talk about my plans for the grounds?" Lori asked in a rather desperate attempt to return the conversation to safer territory. They were getting too close too fast.

"No. Lori?" Shade's voice dropped to a husky whisper. "I'm not very good at playing games. I'd like to be honest with you about a lot of things. About what I'm feeling."

No. She wasn't ready for that. If she started talking, she might say things better kept to herself. This man was awakening emotions, feelings, she didn't understand. "I have plans for the place," she said with more strength than she felt.

Shade sighed. "All right. We'll play the game your way. Today. What are we going to do to this jungle? You don't suppose Tarzan really is hiding out in here, do you?"

Lori ignored what she felt was an attempt to tease her and launched a rapid-fire outline of her need to develop a site analysis that would include property boundaries, structures, fences, walls, natural features, even weather information. "An irrigation system is going to be a major consideration," she pointed out, trying to deny the fact that Shade was concentrating on her eyes and not the gestures she was making with her hands. "I'd like to get rid of all those garden hoses. I want to put in underground sprinkler systems. That way visitors can concentrate on the grounds, not dodging hoses. It'd be easier for them to mentally transport themselves to a historic setting."

"Good point. I'll set up a meeting with our budget director." Shade reached out a hand as if to touch her, but when she shied away, he drew back. "You spent your weekend planning things, didn't you?"

Lori relaxed a little. She didn't know what to make of his slightly wistful tone, but it sounded as if Shade was turning his attention to their reason for being here. Good. That was the way things had to be. "What are there in the way of photographic records?" she asked, not yet trusting herself to turn toward him.

"You are serious about conducting business, aren't you?" Shade asked slowly. "I can help you with that. The museum has a rather extensive collection of photographs of the farm. Also, I'm sure Ruth's family photographs will help. Speaking of Ruth—" Shade paused a moment before going on. "I think she probably has her lipstick on now. Would you like to meet her?"

Lori nodded. "I still can't get over the idea that she'd turn her home over to the historical society. That's a tremendous sacrifice."

"Sacrifice nothing," Shade laughed as he took Lori's elbow and steered her toward the house. "Ruth just likes company. This is her way of ensuring that there'll be people around all the time."

Lori wished there was some polite way she could tell Shade that she was capable of making it to the house without his guidance, but Shade Ryan seemed to feel that physical contact was part and parcel of the conversation. It wasn't that she didn't like being touched by him; it was just that his fingers caressing her flesh made it hard for her to concentrate on the business at hand. She suspected he knew that, which made it even harder for her to ignore the pressure on her elbow.

As they neared the wooden steps leading to the front door, Lori heard an elderly feminine voice calling to them. She turned to the right, to the side of the house, which had a screen-enclosed side porch. Inside was an older woman sitting in a rocker next to a small wooden table.

"Bring her over here, Shade," Ruth commanded. "So you've hired a woman. I should have known."

"Don't let anything Ruth says shock you," Shade whispered. His breath chased a fiery path down the side of Lori's neck. "Ruth likes nothing better than to tease me."

A moment later Shade was opening the screen door and letting Lori in ahead of him. She pulled away from him and forced herself to focus on her hostess and not the sensation still teasing her neck.

If Lori was expecting lavender and old lace, she was in for a disappointment. Ruth Kadin was dressed in a very up-to-date slacks-and-blouse outfit. The red blouse with its V-neck opening and soft collar added to the color in her cheeks. Ruth's silver hair had recently been professionally styled. Her hands, with their arthritis-swollen knuckles, were clutching an oversize mug filled with steaming coffee. She nodded at two wicker chairs near her. "Sit down, you two. I'd have you in, but your shoes are wet from the dew. I've told you before, Shade, I won't have you and your people messing up my house."

"We're not interested in the house, and you know it, Ruth," Shade shot back as he rather gingerly tested the chair's ability to hold his weight. "You just don't like being inside yourself; admit it."

"Don't get smart with me, young man. Have some coffee."

Silently, Lori picked up a mug identical to Ruth's. She knew how to take an order, especially with the smell of freshly ground coffee teasing her senses. She took a small sip and waited to see what direction the conversation was going to take.

It didn't take long for her to have her answer. "I've just dug out some of the old account books my father kept," Ruth explained. "You might find it interesting to see what he paid for the fruit trees behind the house. I have some seed and nursery catalogs my sister left here. Shade doesn't understand gardening enough to know what he's looking at, but you, my dear, should."

Lori wasn't sure whether that was a suggestion or an order, but she found Ruth too delightful to take offense. "They sound fascinating," she responded. "I don't know if Mr. Ryan told you, but I've done several historic garden restorations. When it comes to land-scaping, they're my first love."

"Shade hasn't told me anything about you. The man seems to think it's none of my business who he lets come on my property. Are you married?"

Lori blinked at the unexpected question, but Shade was calmly sipping coffee. "I'm divorced," she said briefly. "I just moved here."

"Shade's divorced, too. It gives you two a lot in common."

"I'm not sure about that," Lori said, already won-dering if anything she'd say would change this deter-mined woman's mind. Obviously she didn't believe in keeping her opinions to herself. "Just because we've both had an unsuccessful marriage—"

"Nonsense! You've both learned what you did wrong the first time. You know how to make it work the second time."

"I'm not so sure about that, either," Lori whispered, taking comfort in the warm liquid flowing down her throat.

An unbelievably soft hand closed over Lori's. "I'm sorry, my dear. I had no right saying what I did. Some-times I let my age be an excuse for taking more liber-ties than I should. It's just that when I see two attractive young people alone, I want to see them happy. I was married to the same old goat for over fifty years. It wasn't all one honeymoon by any means, but it cer-tainly beats being alone."

Lori found herself warming to Ruth Kadin. "I'm not taking offense," she said honestly. "The truth is I don't mind being alone. In fact, I like my own com-pany. I'm a loner."

"So am I. Now. But I don't prefer it this way. So tell me, my dear, what do you think of this man?"

Lori gave up. Obviously the elderly woman wasn't about to be sidetracked from her matchmaking attempts. "He's not what I expected of a museum director," she said, hoping it was a reply that wouldn't get her into trouble.

Ruth laughed. "You can say that again. If I was thirty years younger—what do you think? Shade. Do you like older women?"

Shade gave Ruth a long-suffering look that was so transparent Lori had to fight to keep a straight face. "Ruth, I'd never be able to keep up with you," he said. "How are you this morning? The arthritis giving you any trouble?"

Ruth snorted. "You don't want to talk about my arthritis, and I sure as hell don't. I want to hear all about this beautiful young woman who is going to transform my farm into a thing of beauty. However did you get to be whatever it is you call yourself."

"A horticulturist," Lori supplied, and then launched into a short description of her education and background, not mentioning that her partner in her previous business was her ex-husband. Shade was right. Ruth Kadin was far from the stereotype of the sweet little old lady. "There were certain things I was ready to put behind me," she wound up. "I wanted a change of operation."

Ruth sipped her coffee. "Did you guess you'd have such an incredible hunk of a man for your boss? Are you sure you're too young for me, Shade? I promise not to hold your lack of experience against you."

Shade laughed and gently patted Ruth's hand. "Let me give it some thought, Ruth. I might just take you up on your offer."

"Offer, nothing. I'm propositioning you, young man."

"In that case—" Shade got to his feet "—I think it's time I went to work. I know when I'm in over my head. Lori, I've got to get back to the museum, but maybe Ruth can show you some of the old records." His eyes lingered on Lori's face longer than they needed to.

"Coward," Ruth taunted as Shade left. Then she turned toward Lori. "I love that man. He makes me feel so alive. What do you think of him?"

"He—he's interesting," Lori answered lamely, because anything else might give Ruth even more encouragement to pursue a subject Lori wasn't ready for. Then, because further conversation seemed indicated, she explained that he'd served as her guide around the farm the other night. "He didn't seem to mind the rain at all."

"I'm delighted that you're going to be around, my dear," Ruth said seriously. "Let me tell you something in confidence, and then I'll show you those old records. Shade has come a long way in the past few months. The divorce was very hard on him. He convinced himself that he was responsible for everything that went wrong. He let that woman take him to the cleaners because he was so concerned about her. He's that way about people. He cares. I told him he had better stop stewing and attend to business. Thank heavens he's been doing that. Now maybe you're the woman to help him get his personal life back in order."

"I don't think so, Ruth," Lori said, revealing more than she thought she was going to. "I'm not good wife material."

"I think you're wrong. You're not giving yourself enough credit. Do you know what I see when I look at you? I see a woman with a great deal of love to give."

Lori swallowed something that came dangerously

close to tears. She hadn't thought about love's role in her life for so long that the possibility was something she wasn't ready to handle. "I'll think about that" was the best she could do.

"Do more than think about it, my dear," Ruth said softly. "I've had over eighty years now to study people. I'm not often wrong. And I've been a widow for ten years now. It's a poor substitute for having someone to share my life with."

I'm sorry for you, Lori thought. *But you and I aren't the same person. I'm too much like my father. I'm better off with my own company.*

Chapter Four

Ruth, who insisted Lori call her by her first name, brought a cardboard box onto the enclosed porch and started going through it. Although the elderly woman occasionally digressed with stories about long-dead relatives, she was Lori's best possible source of information about the farm's history. The box contained everything from land records and deeds to sketches and photographs of garden plots Ruth's husband had made. The sketches were designed to mark the outlines of crops but included considerable detail about the fences and hedges used to mark boundaries between the house and garden and fields.

"What are you going to do with all this?" Ruth asked after offering to let Lori take the box with her. "I know, I know. Shade says now that I've given the land to the historical society, I have to trust them. But I can't help but be curious. You aren't going to bring a tractor in here, are you?"

"Hardly," Lori reassured her. "Except for some tree-trimming equipment to cut out the mistletoe, everything's going to be done with hand labor. In fact, I'll be doing a lot of the work myself. I wouldn't think of letting a tractor in where vines and flowers could be crushed. Ruth, this place was a labor of love for you for years. I want that to show when we're done.''

Ruth sighed and got to her feet. "I have to make some phone calls, so I'm going to let you go back to work. But I'm delighted Shade hired a woman. I think it takes a woman to understand how much the hothouse and rose garden mean to me. Even those irises have memories, although the darn things push out everything around them.''

"I hope I can live up to your confidence," Lori said as she, too, got to her feet.

"You will, my dear. I can see it in your eyes," she said, giving Lori's hand a pat before going inside.

Lori left the shade of the enclosed porch and stepped back outside. In the hour she'd been talking to Ruth, the day had warmed considerably. A couple of workmen had arrived to repair the fundation of the old barn. She placed the cardboard box in her Mustang and then wandered over to watch them work. Although she wasn't an expert in building construction, she could see that the four-by-fours that served as the barn's foundation had surrendered to assault from the elements and would have to be replaced. She wondered whether work on the barn and other outbuildings would be completed before she'd done what she had been hired to do.

That question brought up the weightier one of what she was going to do with her life after she was done with the Kadin farm. If she was her father, she'd simply pack up her belongings and move on to the next challenge. But leaving the area would mean leaving Shade Ryan.

Lori tore herself away from her thoughts. She would think about planning the rest of her life in a few weeks, after she'd mapped out what she'd been hired to accomplish.

Lori spent the morning taking notes of the types of plants that grew on the farm. She identified honeysuckle, trumpet vine, rhododendron, aster, holly, English ivy, periwinkle, even several jade plants in the greenhouse. Although ash and walnut trees predominated, she found a willow tree, several apple and fig trees and, behind the tower, a chokecherry. She supplemented her notes with sketches of various sections of the land, such as what grew around the springhouse, the layout of the rose garden, the overgrown flower garden that marked the boundary between house and lawn. By the time the workmen were taking their lunch break, Lori had done as much as she could without a camera. She got into her car and drove over to the museum. Talking to Shade or the financial director about her budget was something she had to do before she bought so much as a roll of film.

Lori was informed that although Shade was having a luncheon meeting with members of the historical-society board, she could go into the conference room. She felt hesitant about interrupting the meeting, but she really was stymied until she could talk to Shade again. Hopefully, he'd understand that, and not read anything into the fact that she was seeing him twice in one day.

The meeting she walked in on was much less formal than she expected. Shade and three middle-aged men were eating sack lunches around a small table. Their sandwiches shared space with a large blueprint spread over the table. Shade looked up, his gaze lingering on her longer than Lori thought necessary.

"Gentlemen, this is our new landscaping expert,"

Shade said, stretching a powerful arm in Lori's direction. "I'm breaking her in on the Kadin farm. If she proves herself there, we might have enough to keep her busy for the next ten years."

Lori's mouth dropped open. This was the first she'd heard that. "Am I interrupting something?" she asked tentatively. "Your secretary said it was all right if—"

"Fine. Fine. You want something to eat?" Shade held out an orange.

Lori shook her head. "I've come about my budget."

"Your budget?" Shade looked disappointed. "I suppose, if you insist. Are you sure you wouldn't like to stay here and hear about the new research library we're going to build?"

Again, Lori shook her head. "I could come back later," she offered. The way the three men were staring at her was making her uncomfortable. She knew it came from spending so much time in her own company, but she'd never felt at ease in a group, especially if she was the only woman.

"No need." Shade reached for a nearby telephone. "I'll see if Frederick's in the building. He's the one you'll need to see. Are you sure you don't want this orange?"

A minute later Shade had arranged for Lori to go to the second floor of the museum where the financial director's office was. "Lori?" he called as she was getting ready to leave. When she turned around, he tossed the orange her way. "I have to look after your best interests. Frederick will talk your leg off. This'll help keep your strength up."

Four long hours later Lori had to agree that the orange had been her salvation. Frederick Harper was a stickler for detail. He made sure Lori understood every aspect of the federal grant that was making the farm-restoration project possible. He also seemed to feel it was necessary for Lori to understand the entire financial base of the historical society. By the time she'd been given a ledger for record keeping and vouchers allowing her to draw from a special account, Lori felt as if she'd crammed a semester-long accounting course into an afternoon. She felt somewhat light-headed and yet suffered from a headache as a result of spending all that time in a small office without adequate ventilation.

When she was finally released, Lori sought the museum's grounds the way a child runs for a playground at recess. She leaned against one of the willows that shaded the grounds and breathed deeply, trying to rid her lungs of smoke and stale air. Her stomach rumbled loudly.

When her head had cleared enough to allow her to think, Lori made her way to the employee parking lot and started to unlock her car. That's when she heard her name being called.

"Are you still alive?" Shade asked as he strolled toward her, swinging a briefcase lightly in one hand. "I should have warned you."

"I feel as if I spent the day in school. He's so thorough," Lori admitted. She shouldn't feel this much better simply because her boss was talking to her, but she did.

"Well," Shade said, tossing his briefcase in the back seat of his Camaro, "school's over. Now's the best time of the day. What do you want to do? Go down to the malt shops? Kids don't go to malt shops anymore, do they? I think they go to video arcades."

Lori pressed a hand to her forehead, trapping her hair against her scalp. "My head would never stand an arcade. I need peace and quiet." How dare he look so alive, so vibrant, when she felt as if she'd just stepped out of a sweatshop.

"Now where can we find some peace and quiet? I've got it." Shade snapped his fingers. "I know just the place." If she'd been thinking like a child racing for the swings, then Shade was the boy already pumping his legs as he worked his body skyward.

"We?" Lori asked. "The only thing I'm interested in is going home and opening a can of soup."

"I'll go along with the idea of going home, but I'm going to veto soup. Can't you cook anything else?"

"Of course!" Lori snapped, and was instantly sorry she'd taken offense. He was obviously enjoying the fact that it was 5:00 P.M. She shouldn't put a damper on his enthusiasm. "I just don't want to bother with anything else for myself."

"Who said anything about yourself? In case you weren't listening, I just invited myself along."

"What? You can't—" She couldn't imagine him wanting to spend time with someone who felt like something the cat dragged in.

"Why can't I?" he pressed, his grin determined. "It's my house."

Shade's statement stopped her. Of course it was his house. "I'm sorry," she relented. "Are you sure you want to go there? I mean, I thought you didn't like—"

"You thought I didn't like the house because of the memories associated with it." Shade frowned. He took a step closer and lowered his voice. He wasn't sure how wise it was to tell Lori how much her presence had changed him already, but the wanting to was stronger than caution. "I didn't think I did, either," he said with an honesty that surprised him. "But I spent the weekend thinking about you being in it and decided it was time to look at things from a different perspective. I hope you don't mind my suggestion. I've spent today talking to what seems like a thousand people. I'd like to go somewhere where the only sound other than your voice is the wind in the trees.''

Shade did look tired. Lori had been thinking so much about her own discomfort that she hadn't noticed that. Now that he was no longer holding on to his briefcase, his arms were sagging at his side. Whether it was an act or his true state was too complicated to decide. "I'm afraid all I can offer is soup," she relented. "I've never taken much interest in shopping for one."

"Do you have eggs?"

"Of course, but—"

"But nothing. Look, I'm going to stop by a deli and pick up some cheese and meats, and then we'll put together one of the world's greatest omelets. Why don't you go on ahead and open the house, set a table on the deck?"

Lori could have said no, but she didn't. She thought about spending the evening on the balcony breathing in the scent of pines and feeling the wind in her hair. She wanted to share that with someone, with Shade.

When she reached the house, Lori did as Shade suggested. She opened the sliding-glass door, mixed up some instant ice tea and wiped off the glass-top table on the deck before getting out silverware and plates. She'd kicked off her shoes and was padding around on the thick carpet of the living room when Shade walked in.

For an instant the strangest feeling reached Lori. They looked like a married couple, husband coming home from work to find the wife preparing dinner. The only thing that didn't fit the picture was that Shade was bringing in a bag of groceries and walking toward the kitchen without giving his wife a welcoming kiss.

"If we don't get some board members who don't smoke—" Shade didn't finish his sentence. He stared down at Lori's feet and then smiled. "That's the best idea I've seen all day." His instincts were right. Deciding to have dinner with Lori was the best idea he'd had all day. He was too tired to ponder the pros and cons of having a personal relationship with an employee. He was too tired to do anything but share an hour or two with a woman who touched him with energy even though he'd managed to hold off the desire to take her in his arms. He leaned over, untied his shoes and gave his feet a healthy kick that sent his shoes crashing against the far wall of the kitchen. "Whoever invented shoes was a sadist."

Lori climbed up on a stool and watched as Shade moved about the kitchen, opening the refrigerator and selecting condiments for the omelet. "You're very domestic," she observed, feeling relaxed and comfortable about what was happening. She'd been wrong. Spending the evening alone wasn't what she wanted to do, after all.

"I learned to be," Shade was saying. "Vicky wasn't much of a cook. I'm still not sure she could open a can of soup."

"I assure you, I can do more than that," Lori said, not knowing why she felt she should compare herself with Shade's ex-wife. "Have you told her about my living here?"

Shade shook his head. "Despite transatlantic calls, it's very hard to track down someone on a European tour. I wasn't too crazy about Vicky taking off like that. She has almost no money sense. She's too trusting of strangers.''

Lori swiped a piece of tomato before it could go into the omelet and popped it into her mouth. "You have to let her live her own life.''

Shade's head came up. There was something in his eyes that set Lori's nerves on edge. "You're not the first person to tell me that,'' he said sharply. "However, it's something I can deal with on my own.''

"I'm sorry,'' Lori relented. "You're right. I didn't mean—''

"I know Vicky a lot better than anyone else. A hell of a lot better than her parents did. They were only too glad to have one more mouth out of the house. They didn't stop to see if they were sending a child out to be a wife.'' Shade stopped, frowned and then attacked the cheese he was grating. "It was a mistake,'' he said softly. "I wasn't what Vicky needed, what she wanted.''

"You don't have to talk about it,'' Lori said just as softly. She didn't feel particularly comfortable talking about Shade's problems, but she was grateful for the honesty that was taking place. "Rehashing the reasons behind a divorce doesn't change anything.''

Shade looked at her for a long minute. His green eyes seemed capable of probing deep in her soul. "You're right. Look, I brought a bottle of wine. Why don't you pour us a couple of glasses?''

Lori came within a breath of saying no. Shade might be seeing tonight simply as a way for two tired people to share a meal without having to go to a restaurant, but Lori wasn't sure she could keep things in that perspective. Not only was she aware of the way Shade dominated the kitchen, but whenever she looked into his eyes, she forgot that theirs was an employer-employee relationship. Wine was something friends or lovers shared.

But she couldn't tell Shade that. Maybe to his way of thinking wine was as natural an accompaniment to a meal as ice tea. If she said something about reading anything of an intimate nature into wine, he might think she wanted something even more personal to take place.

Lori buried her thoughts by casually reaching for a couple of wineglasses and then telling Shade a little about the time she'd spent with Ruth.

"You have permission to run rampant through the museum tomorrow," he said. "Alice Cartright is the head of the research library. She knows the photographic records like the back of her hand. She can get you what you need much faster than I could."

"That's fine," Lori said as she took her first sip of dry white wine. "I wouldn't want to take up your time."

"There's nothing I'd like better." Shade poured the egg mix into a hot skillet and picked up his own wineglass. He lifted his glass in her direction in a wordless toast. "I have to spend tomorrow with those same board members. I smell like an ashtray."

Lori hadn't gotten close enough to Shade to notice that, but as he moved about, putting away the leftover ingredients, she found herself breathing deeper than usual, needing now to find out what he did smell like. The smoke was there, but so, too, was an undeniable hint of masculinity. For a moment she thought she might lose herself in that smell. "Do you mind working indoors?" she asked in order to bring her thoughts around in a safer direction. "I mean, you obviously love being out at the farm. Does it bother you that you have to wear a suit and tie?" Lori, who seldom tried to get into another person's head, wanted an honest answer from Shade Ryan.

"I don't wear a tie any more than I have to. And no, I don't really mind. Like I said, I like people. Right now, though, there's just one person I want to be around. Can I tell you something? It was thinking of you that got me through the day." Shade had moved a step closer to where Lori sat. His expression said that his revelation wasn't a casual statement.

Despite herself, Lori dropped her eyes.

"Look at me."

"What?" She raised her head.

"I said, look at me. I was saying something nice about an attractive young woman. I didn't say it to hear myself talk. Accept the compliment."

"I don't think of myself as attractive," Lori admitted, wondering at her ability to be so open about herself to this man. "My father always said that the only really important thing a person has to offer to the world is his or her brain."

"The ERA would love your father. He's right, of course, but there's more to people than brains." Shade reached out and touched the tip of Lori's nose. "There are emotions, feelings, the ability to express sensitivity. I'd like to learn more about what makes your heart beat."

This time Lori did blush, although not out of embarrassment. She wasn't used to intimate conversation and sought some way of pulling back. "My heart's no different from anyone else's," she managed.

"Don't be so sure, Lori." There was still distance

between Lori and Shade, but it seemed to disappear as he spoke. "There's a lot to you. I don't think your real emotions have been tapped yet."

Lori swallowed, and stifled an impulse to touch him in gratitude. The moment was electric with potential, but it would be dangerous to explore that potential. She knew enough about her body to realize how close she was to surrendering to his maleness. "Maybe I'm not interested in sharing that."

"I don't believe you. No one should keep everything boarded up inside them."

Lori shook her head. She was dangerously off balance and knew how much strength it would take to keep the moment from becoming more than she could handle. "Don't do this to me, Shade," she begged. "I don't know how to talk about myself. I'm not comfortable doing it."

"What are you comfortable with?" Shade turned to tend the omelet, but his words followed her, not letting go of the conversation.

"What I do," Lori replied, surprised at her willingness to admit that. "I'm proud of the work I do."

"That's good." Shade handed her one of the plates. "But it isn't enough. Maybe—" He stopped for a minute. "I'm going too fast. I'm sorry. Do you think we need anything else with this?"

Lori studied the mountain of eggs on her plate. She wasn't quite sure what he meant by going too fast but accepted the change to a safer topic. "Not for me. I'm not sure I can eat this much."

"All set." Shade turned off the stove and picked up his plate. "Let's go out on the deck. Fresh air. It's great for an appetite. I always eat like a horse when I go camping."

They ate in silence for several minutes, sharing eggs and wine and a brisk wind. Lori followed Shade's lead by leaning back in her lawn chair and balancing her plate on her lap. She stretched out her legs and wriggled her toes, feeling the tension of a minute ago evaporate. It was almost as if she hadn't had that silent war with her emotions. Maybe it was the wine talking, but she decided that this ability to simply enjoy a quiet dinner with another person was what life was about.

"What are you thinking about?" Shade asked abruptly.

"What?" Lori looked up from her meal. "I wasn't aware I was thinking about anything."

"You must have been. Your eyes were kind of glazed over, and you weren't even blinking. That's a sign of deep thoughts."

Lori lowered her lids to shade her eyes. "I was thinking about how peaceful this is. Thank you. You had the perfect suggestion."

"It was easy." The deep masculine rumble came from deep in Shade's chest and instantly altered Lori's relaxed state. "I took one look at you and decided this is what we both needed tonight. Does it bother you, having your boss cook dinner?"

"Should it?" She breathed deeply, slowly, in order to keep her thoughts locked safely inside.

"No." Shade tossed back his head and laughed. "The ERA would love me, too. I figure that when two people want to share something, it doesn't matter who does what. It's the being together that counts. I hope you feel the same way."

Lori admitted that she did. Except for her father, she couldn't remember ever feeling this alive around another person. True, he was her boss. But it was evening. They were two people sharing a meal on a deck overlooking a valley. "If I ever get rich, I want a place like this," she said, breaking the silence. "Not the house exactly but the surroundings. I can't think of anything more perfect."

"Do you want to buy the place?" Shade frowned. "I didn't mean that. I guess I still have a lot of unresolved feelings about it."

Lori felt she understood what Shade was feeling, but she didn't feel she knew him well enough to press him to explore his emotions. Besides, she didn't know enough about opening up herself. She didn't know how to get another person to do that. She'd been supporting herself since high school. Because she had to work, it had taken her five years to get through college, but she didn't mind. When she graduated, she had a firm grasp of what she wanted to do with her life and what she was going to have to do to accomplish it.

Her career was established. It was her personal life that wasn't going in traditional directions.

When they finished eating, Lori cleared the table and washed the dishes. She returned to the deck to find that Shade had turned on the stereo; the sounds of songs from the 1970s were reaching the deck from the living room. Shade stretched back in his lawn chair and propped his feet up on the deck railing.

"I have a strange way of looking at music," he explained as she sat down. "I decide I like a song long after it has faded from the charts." He closed his eyes and let his head rest against the chair top. "I was living in California when that song was popular. It was summer." He was silent for a minute. "I'd taken a leave of absence from a research project I was doing for the federal government and spent a month on the coast at

Point Sur. That was before I met Vicky. Looking back, I think that summer was one of the most peaceful times of my life. I grew a beard, ran around in sandals, did everything except learn to surf. I doubt if I knew two people by name at Point Sur, but that didn't bother me."

"It didn't?" Lori looked over at Shade, thankful for the opportunity to study him while his eyes were closed. The lines on his face were so faint as to be almost nonexistent. His depth came from what he was capable of feeling. "I thought you liked being around people."

"I do. Most of the time. But all of us need time alone to get in touch with our thoughts. I did a lot of thinking about my career and decided to look for something that offered more challenge." He laughed low in his throat. "I certainly did that. I became director of a historical society. And I got married. What about you?" Shade slowly opened his eyes. "I take it you came here because you needed to get away from an uncomfortable situation. Have you come to any momentous decisions about your life?"

"I made the biggest decision of my life when I decided I wasn't cut out to be a wife," Lori said with more candor than she thought she was capable of. "I wasn't good for Brett. The best thing I could do for him was let him go on with his life, find a woman who needed him."

"You didn't need him?"

Lori shifted uncomfortably in her chair but couldn't think of any graceful way of getting out of the conversation she'd started. She could hardly tell Shade that what she wanted was for him to talk about himself, not her past. "I don't know if that's the right way to put it," she said slowly, softly. "There were good times. I don't want you to think it was all bad. But Brett likes to be surrounded by people. I prefer being alone."

"You aren't alone now. Does that make you uncomfortable?"

Lori turned and met Shade's jade eyes. She sensed that he wasn't seeking an answer that would simply satisfy his ego. He honestly wanted to know what she was feeling. "No," she whispered, not feeling the need to draw a curtain over what her eyes might be revealing. "I like this, sitting here talking to you."

"Then you need people, Lori. We all do."

She turned away from him and looked back at the wilderness surrounding them. The sun was in the process of setting. The trees were dark, fathomless shadows, while the sky was still cloaked in a rose hue. With Brett she was always on stage, trying to fit the mold he'd planned for her. Brett didn't understand long silences or the need to take time to watch the sun set. Shade wouldn't be sitting out here if he didn't have that kind of a need. "I don't know," she whispered, the mountain breeze taking her words. "Maybe I need to spend a month at Point Sur."

"I'm glad you aren't."

"Why?"

"Because we wouldn't be sitting here having this conversation." Shade was quiet for a minute. "What do you say? Do you think we should call a halt to deep subjects for the evening? I have to keep my brain at top speed all day. At night I like to kick back and talk about things like whether the fishing is going to be any good this fall."

Lori laughed, a relaxed glow spreading through her. "What about the fishing? Black Bob and I did a lot of fly-fishing in mountain streams. I know how to tie my own flies. In fact, I have a few tricks that really bring in the big ones.''

"You're going to be a mighty handy person to have around." Shade stretched, groaned and got to his feet. "I hate to say this, but I'm not going to be awake in ten minutes if I stay here. That's a hell of a thing to say to a delightful dinner companion, but I'm afraid it's the truth. I think I'd better go home. I also think I'd like to go fishing with you someday.''

Lori got to her feet, too. It was getting cool outside. No matter how much she'd like to sit here and wait for the moon to come up, she wouldn't be able to do it without getting some kind of wrap.

She watched Shade reach for his keys. It wasn't until he'd started for the door that she realized he was really going. "Do you have to leave?" she heard herself asking. "I could fix us some coffee."

Shade stopped. "Don't tempt me, young lady. No, I don't want any coffee. I'll be up half the night." He turned toward her. "Thank you for a very pleasant evening.''

"Thank you for dinner.''

Lori saw his hand reaching for the back of her head and felt the pressure that brought her closer to him. She could have resisted and put an end to what she sensed coming. But she didn't. Instead, she let him draw her into the circle of his arms.

Lori stood with his arms wrapped around her shoulders and back, looking up into his eyes. There were tiny laugh lines radiating out from the outer corners of his eyes, lines that said something about a man who enjoyed life. She wondered if she was expected to say something. She'd already thanked him for dinner. The words in her heart were much too fragile to be exposed for anyone to hear.

Because silence was more comfortable than words, Lori continued to stand looking up at him, studying the waves and curls of his too-long hair, feeling his heart beating in the chest an inch away from hers.

Shade opened his mouth. She thought he was going to say something. Instead, the corners of his eyes crinkled and his mouth softened.

Lori was ready for his kiss. She had seen it coming and made an instantaneous decision to let it happen. As he pulled her against his muscled chest and reached for her lips, Lori let her lids slide down over her eyes, surrendering to the sensation of being in a man's arms in a darkened living room. Behind them the stereo was playing a love song that had been popular when she was in college. It reminded her of ivy-covered buildings, football games, evenings spent in a library cramming for a test. Because she worked, Lori hadn't been part of the college life that revolved around love songs. Now, finally, she realized how much she had missed that.

But there was a second time, a chance to touch an old memory. Shade's lips were soft on hers, his arms a warm blanket on her chilled flesh. For the first time Lori was able to experience the love ballad as it had been meant to be experienced.

Her arms sought Shade's waist. She wrapped them around him to keep from losing her balance—and to hold on to the sensation that existed somewhere between past and present. If it was ten years ago they might be walking hand in hand to one of their dorms, a college football game, the library.

This wasn't ten years ago. The song was a tie to the past, but their kiss was very much part of the present.

"I didn't know I was going to do that," Shade whispered. His voice wasn't as confident as she remembered it. "I really thought I was going to be able to walk out of here without kissing you."

"That's all right," Lori said from the depths of his embrace. "I don't mind."

Lori felt his arms tighten around her. "I've never done that before. I want you to know that. I've never tried to take advantage of an employee."

An employee. That's what she was, she tried to remind herself. "I believe you. It must be the music."

"No," Shade whispered. "It was the company."

He was releasing her. She could feel his hands start to pull away. Then, almost convulsively, he drew her against him again, his mouth searching. Although it made no sense and went against all logic, Lori offered him what he was looking for. This time she knew his eyes were closed, too.

His heart vibrating against her chest became stronger. The sensation told her of his vibrancy, his life. Strange, she'd never heard another human's heart like this before.

The thought lasted only an instant. It was much more important not to think at all, to simply absorb sensations. Lori seldom gave thought to her size, but now she felt small and protected and very, very safe. It didn't make sense. She shouldn't be standing here kissing her boss, but she had no desire to end what was happening.

Shade was the one who pulled away. "I'm going to let you go," he said raggedly. "I'm going to walk out that door and not look back."

He was true to his word. Lori stood watching him leave, her body suddenly hungry and lonely and chilled. She didn't try to understand what was happening to her until his car lights came on and he drove away.

Lori closed the door and leaned against it, staring at the dark living room. Had she really just left her boss's arms, she wondered. It had felt so right, so natural, while it was happening, but now there was something almost mystical about the memory.

That's what you get for drinking wine and watching the sun set with the stereo on, Lori told herself as she turned on a lamp and went about locking up for the night. *I just hope he realizes we were both caught up in the same mood. The kiss didn't mean anything.*

By the time she was ready for bed, Lori had just about convinced herself that the evening's mood and nothing else was responsible for what had happened. The only thing she didn't quite understand was why she let the stereo continue to play old songs until she was ready to climb into bed.

Chapter Five

Lori stood on the lawn, looking out toward the road, or rather what she could see of the road through the underbrush. She had a clipboard in her hands and was alternately making sketches and looking at her surroundings. In the back pocket of her jeans were the just-developed pictures she'd taken of the farm.

It was a distractingly clear day, but Lori was barely aware of that fact. Foremost in her mind was that the farm was to be made accessible to visitors and thus major walkways had to be established while retaining the grounds' unique flavor. She'd decided to allow visitors to come up to the front of the springhouse but to stop them there. If they were able to walk around the low stone structure, that would destroy much of the English ivy that crawled up the rock sides and stretched along the slope leading to the springhouse. She'd been relieved to hear that a parking area would be established at the entrance to the farm and thus no heavy clearing near the house would take place.

She was only vaguely aware of a screen door opening behind her and jumped when Ruth called her name.

"Oh, my dear, you were lost in thought, weren't

you," Ruth said as she stood holding on to the door. "Are you terribly busy?"

Lori pressed a hand to her forehead and grimaced. "Not if I can help it. I think I'm getting brain drain from all this thinking. Is there something I can do for you?"

"I hope so. I'd like to walk out to the barn and see the work that's being done, but I don't trust my legs."

"Of course." Lori tucked her pencil in her back pocket and laid her clipboard on the ground. "I've been looking for an excuse to poke around there myself. Let me help you down the stairs."

Lori was bothered by how much Ruth relied on her strength to help her out of the screened porch and down onto the grass, but didn't say anything. Instead, she complimented Ruth on her bright green sweater and the matching slacks that set off her still-slender body. "I've been so busy the past few days," Lori said. "I'm sorry I haven't come by and thanked you again for the coffee."

"No thanks are necessary, and I know how busy you've been. I watched you taking pictures the other day. Did you get what you needed?"

Lori assured the elderly woman that she now had a complete record of the farm's present condition. "I should have a complete set of the historical pictures from the museum by this afternoon," she explained. "Now that I've made a preliminary determination of what needs to be done to restore the grounds to what the pictures show, I'll be getting together with Shade this afternoon." She shook her head at the sudden thought. "I'm eager to get started. It's probably a good thing I have to get approval before I jump into things."

"You haven't seen Shade lately? I don't understand that man." Ruth pursed her lips as they started down the gravel road leading to the barn. "I don't know what I'm going to have to do to make him aware of the fact that there's an attractive woman under his nose. He can keep his nose to the grindstone only so long."

He's aware of me, Lori thought, but kept the thought to herself. Instead she said something about both of them being very busy and then guided the conversation around until Ruth was telling her how her father and two other farmers had built the impressive barn in less than a month. As they stood outside the barn's entrance and stared up at the exposed rafters, Lori tried to put herself in Ruth's father's position. Today when someone needed a barn built, they contracted to have the work done and hurried the job along with the aid of modern equipment. She had no idea how three men had managed to build a three-story barn without jeopardizing life and limb. She could only hope that visitors to the farm would appreciate that basic fact.

Ruth breathed heavily for a minute. "My doctor tells me I should move where there aren't any stairs. The crazy man. I can't leave here."

"Ruth, maybe he has a point," Lori started hesitantly. She hated saying anything, but there was no ignoring how much Ruth depended on her for balance. "Is there any way you can have one of those stair elevators installed in your house? It might make it easier for you to get around."

"I'm not putting any damn elevator in my house! When we're done here, I'll show you the inside. It'd ruin everything I hold dear about the place to put in one of those contraptions."

Lori bit her tongue. Obviously Ruth had made up

her mind about that matter. And yet Lori couldn't help but worry. Ruth lived alone. If she fell, she would be without help for a long time. Maybe it was something she could talk to Shade about.

"I'm dying to see if the barn owls have any babies," Ruth said as they entered the cool, open barn interior. "We've had owls nesting here for close to forty years. I told Shade I'd have his workmen kicked out on their ears if they did anything to disturb my owls."

Lori giggled at the idea of Ruth's giving Shade a boot but admitted that the woman would probably try to make good on her threat. "Where are the owls?" she asked, blinking in an attempt to adjust to the contrast between deep shadows and what light came through the spaces between the barn's side boards. A couple of men were placing heavy jacks under a corner of the barn in preparation for placing a new foundation, but they were being kept company by several curious chickens, not barn owls.

Ruth walked to the middle of the barn and pointed upward. Straight overhead Lori could just make out some kind of platform near the top of one of the main support timbers. "That's where my babies are," Ruth explained. "Darn these old eyes. I can't see a thing. Do you see any movement?"

Lori waited, her neck aching from the unnatural position until she thought she detected a slight movement. As she concentrated, she caught the movement again and then was able to make out the rounded brown head and large stern eyes looking down at her. A thrill of discovery shot through her. "There they are. I see one of them."

"The babies. What about the babies?"

Again Lori concentrated. The shadows at the top of

the barn were so deep that when the owl stopped moving, she couldn't see him, and yet she was sure there was some kind of nest to one side of the platform. Suddenly, with a flurry of wings, another owl joined the first and started dipping its head repeatedly toward the nest. "I think they're feeding the babies," Lori exclaimed, laughing with the joy of her discovery. "I'm sure that's what's happening."

Ruth sighed and laughed with Lori. "I just had to make sure my babies were safe. I have deer that come around the fruit trees and rabbits in the wheat fields, but the barn owls have always been my favorite. My husband and I discovered them together."

Lori lowered her head to look at Ruth. Although the elderly woman was still smiling, her eyes were glistening. Lori put her arm around Ruth's shoulder. "You miss him, don't you?" she said softly.

"Of course I miss the old goat. That's why I won't listen to that fool doctor. I can't leave Jack here alone."

Lori was silent. She understood what Ruth was saying but needed time to think about the deeper truth being expressed. Jack Kadin was dead, but his memory remained at the farm. This was the only true home Ruth had known, where she'd spent fifty years of married life.

"I think that's beautiful," Lori whispered as they walked back out into the sunlight. "Not many people have the kind of memories you do."

"They're precious," Ruth said softly. "Sometimes at night I miss Jack so much I don't think I can stand it, but then day comes, and I see him everywhere I look. I'm very happy then."

"I'm sorry the nights are hard."

"It can't be helped, child; it can't be helped." Ruth

gave her a mischievous wink. "Jack and I made those old bedsprings creak right up until he died. Some people don't believe that. They don't believe a man in his seventies wants to make love to a wrinkled old woman. That's ridiculous! When you love someone, it doesn't matter how old and ugly you are. You still need that kind of closeness."

Lori hurt for Ruth, but when she looked into Ruth's eyes, she saw the light of memories shining back at her, not sorrow. For a minute Lori wasn't sure she could breathe without risking tears herself. What a beautiful, precious relationship Ruth and Jack had had! And how far she was from experiencing what Ruth was telling her.

Ruth had been holding on to Lori's arm, but now she stopped and patted Lori's hand. "What's wrong?"

Lori blinked. "Nothing's wrong. I was just thinking about what you were saying."

"It was more than that, my dear. I see it in your face. There's something terribly sad there. I think you need a man to make love to."

"Ruth!" Lori didn't know whether to laugh or be embarrassed.

"What?" Ruth asked, her own eyes too round and innocent to be believed. "You were married. You have to know what it's like to have a man around whenever you need one."

"I'm afraid I don't." Lori questioned the wisdom of telling Ruth the truth, but she was afraid her eyes would give her away, anyway. "I didn't have that kind of marriage."

"What kind of marriage did you have?"

Lori tried to give Ruth an offended look. "You ask a lot of questions."

"That's one of the privileges of being over eighty. I'm allowed to be as nosy as I want. You didn't like making love?"

"It isn't as simple as that," Lori admitted. Not only wasn't she offended; for some reason Lori was ready to face the question squarely. "Those barn owls? They make love because some instinct tells them to. They don't think about how they both argued over the same mouse or worry over who's going to do most of the work building a nest. Humans mess things up by letting their minds get involved with their bodies."

"You aren't telling me anything," Ruth chided.

Lori waited until she'd gotten Ruth back up the stairs and seated comfortably in her rocker. "I guess I'm not," she admitted. "I tried so hard at first to be the kind of wife Brett wanted. I tried to like parties and noise and sharing everything about my life with him. When I realized that wasn't going to work, I started to resent him. Why couldn't he allow me my own space? Why did I have to be what he wanted?" Lori shook her head. "Even that stopped. Finally, I realized I was the one who was out of step. It wasn't wrong for a person to want to be included in every aspect of his spouse's life. I couldn't help what my upbringing was like or change the reality of never really being close to anyone except my father. I didn't like being asked to share my every thought, my every emotion, and I didn't know how to make myself like that. So I let go."

Ruth had folded her hands peacefully in her lap, but her eyes were anything but peaceful or relaxing to look at. "Your ex-husband sounds like a very insecure man."

"Oh, no," Lori tried to reassure her. "He was a very successful businessman. He knew what he wanted out of life."

"And he wanted you to fit into that life without having any leeway of your own. That, my dear, is insecurity."

Lori stood looking down at Ruth. She'd never thought of it that way before. It simply didn't fit in with what she'd faced when her marriage fell apart. "I'm the one who was the misfit. My father was a cross between a gypsy and a hermit. I take after him."

"Then why are you standing here talking to an old woman? If you were a gypsy or a hermit, you'd have packed your tent and walked on down the road."

Lori had no words to counter what Ruth had said. She was getting a headache from being asked to go back and dig up the remains of a failed marriage. It didn't matter, anyway. She was divorced. Starting over with Brett was the last thing she'd ever attempt. "You're too deep for me, Ruth," she admitted. "I can't keep up with you."

Ruth gave her a long, intense look. "I doubt that. But I do think it's going to take you a while to stop blaming yourself. You have to. Otherwise, you can't get on with your life."

Lori thought Ruth might be too tired to take her on the promised tour of her house, but after resting a few minutes, the older woman insisted on taking her through the ground-floor rooms. "There are three bedrooms upstairs, but two of them are closed off, and I don't go into mine more than once a day," Ruth explained. "That old quack of a doctor is right about one thing. Stairs and I don't get along like we used to."

It didn't bother Lori that she was unable to see the upstairs. She was content to poke through the old-fashioned kitchen with rust stains in the sink, handmade curtains over the dining-nook windows and herbs hanging drying from the low ceiling. Ruth had many of her china dishes out on display, but Lori was afraid to handle them after she learned that they were over a hundred years old. The living room and formal sitting room were constructed with hardwood floors covered with accent rugs that had been made from rags by Ruth and, before her, by her mother.

The furniture went with hardwood floors and faded rugs. Although they were obviously antiques, they were meant to be used and not hidden under dust covers. Lori was afraid to sit in one rocker because the cane backing had frayed in several places. A leg on a coffee table was loose, and the afghan thrown over the back of a couch was obviously there to hide the worn fabric underneath. Lori, who had seen her share of historic homes filled with antiques, was delighted to find a home dedicated to function and not full of hands-off signs. It bothered her to see the accumulation of dust and dirty windows, not because Lori was a stickler for cleanliness but because it was evidence that Ruth was physically unable to keep up with her housework.

Lori didn't say anything, but as she was getting ready to leave, she made her decision. She was going to talk to Shade and see if anything could be done to make it easier for Ruth to stay where she was.

The thought of Shade caused her to glance at the old grandfather's clock in the entry hall. "I had no idea it was so late," she exclaimed. "Shade is going to have my head. I was supposed to meet with him a half hour ago."

"I doubt if he'll lop off your head. It's much too pretty. Besides—" Ruth winked. "Your Mr. Ryan likes you just the way you are."

How do you know, Lori thought, but there wasn't

time to ask. She was the one who had set up the meeting with Shade and the financial director. Her diagram of the traffic-flow pattern wasn't complete, and she hadn't had time to arrange the photographs she'd taken in logical sequence. That plus being late wasn't going to impress anyone.

Lori pushed her old Mustang to the limit of its ability and left it parked haphazardly between two stalls behind the museum. She took the front stairs two at a time and arrived at Shade's outer office out of breath. As she shifted from one foot to the other while she was being announced, Lori ran her fingers across her forehead to push aside the hair she knew would be there. She was sweating! What an impression she was going to make.

Shade was very much aware that Lori was out of breath. He'd been glancing at his watch every few minutes for the last hour, growing both alarmed and impatient because the one person he wanted to see today might not feel the same way. His thoughts were tied up in the memory of a kiss that maybe shouldn't have taken place. Realizing that she'd been rushing gave him an almost boyish confidence. "I was starting to think we'd have to send out a search team for you," Shade said as he came out to usher her in to where the financial director sat glaring at her. "Don't you have a watch?"

Lori shook her head. "They're always getting in the way. I'm sorry. I was talking to Ruth and lost track of time. But I think I have everything I need to make a presentation," she finished up.

Shade said little as she laid out her plans. Although he was still thinking about the last time they were together, he gave no hint. In fact, he was relishing the difference between the woman he held in his arms the other night and the competent businesswoman in front of him today. She had a scale drawing of the present condition of the land to go along with her photographs. Alongside that she placed another drawing of what she envisioned the finished work to look like. With that went the photographs from Ruth.

Lori explained that construction would be limited to reestablishment of the fence that once bordered the south side of the farm where it reached the country road. "I know of several historic gardens around public buildings that have benches and even picnic tables, but I don't feel they'd be right here. We want people to see a farm, not a park."

The financial director continued to frown, but after having spent an afternoon with him, Lori knew that was his demeanor no matter what was being discussed. Shade had followed her presentation intently, his eyes only occasionally leaving the sketches and photographs to stray to her face. "By Jove, Frederick, I think she's got it!" he exclaimed as she waited. Shade asked a few questions about the condition of a couple of diseased trees and the placement of the underground sprinkling system, surprising himself at his ability to isolate business from personal matters. It made him wonder, not for the first time, if it was possible for them to explore both sides of a developing relationship.

The financial director's questions were, Lori thought, minute and picky, but she bit her tongue and answered as completely as possible. She held firm on her insistence that she be allowed to choose the arborist who would do the work on the trees, explaining that a licensed expert was worth whatever they had to pay him. After at least an hour of questions Frederick gave

Shade a short nod. "I can't see any objections to the overall plan. Of course, we have to ask for a strict accounting of any expenditures."

"I'm sure Ms Black is capable of doing that, Frederick," Shade said with a little less patience than he'd shown at the start of the meeting. "Someone who financed her college education is bound to know the value of a dollar."

Lori shot Shade a look of gratitude but said nothing. She'd done the bookkeeping for the business she owned with her husband, but that didn't mean she enjoyed financial details. They were a fact of life, nothing more.

Frederick started to say something about Lori's needing to read the details of the restoration grant, but Shade waved him off. "Let's let her trim her roses or whatever she's going to be doing. I'm sure Lori has enough to do without reading that deadly old document."

"I don't mind," Lori reassured him. "I've never had much to do with grants."

"Then why start now?" Shade interrupted. "You don't have to be an expert in everything, Lori."

Lori bristled. She hadn't expected this from him. "Why not? Are you afraid my head can't handle it?"

"Back up a minute." Shade held up a restraining hand. "I retract that statement. I was just trying to save you some work."

Lori had to admit that he was right. She certainly didn't have to get upset because he was trying to warn her away from what was probably very dull reading material. "Apology accepted." She smiled, her eyes lingering boldly on his lips. It had been a nice kiss—more than nice. "If you'll accept mine. I had no reason to assume you were putting me down."

"I'd never do that, Lori," Shade said softly. "I'm too impressed by what you've done already. Well, Frederick?" He turned toward the financial director. "Can we give her the green light?"

Frederick nodded—reluctantly, it seemed to Lori—and got to his feet. The moment the door had closed behind him, Shade ran his hand over his eyes, groaning. "You'd think every penny was coming out of his pocket. At least we'll never go bankrupt with him at the helm."

Shade helped Lori put away her materials, silence closing around them. Lori knew there was no need for words. He had to be thinking about the last time they were together. It was in the way he let his eyes swing her way, a softening around his mouth. Finally, Shade sighed and patted the neat, if bulging, folder. "I was going to call you last night, see if there were any problems with the house, but I figured you'd holler if the water pipes broke or the electricity went out."

"I'd probably set out candles and wait for morning." It was amazing that they could carry on this conversation with what remained unsaid filling the space between them. "Black Bob and I lived in our share of cabins without electricity."

"A true pioneer. What are you doing tonight?"

"I haven't given it any thought," Lori admitted. "I really do need to wash some clothes."

"Wash them tomorrow. Tonight we're going to see a slide show."

"What?" Lori stared at Shade, but he seemed intrigued by the photograph at the top of the folder of the grape arbor over the house's back door. "I don't want to go to a slide show."

"Too bad." He lifted his head, his eyes saying something entirely different from what was coming from his mouth. "It's one the historical society is sponsoring. It details the history of the lumber industry."

Of course she was interested, interested enough to work her way past the message in his eyes. That was what her father's working life had revolved around. "You should have said that first. I don't like being given orders," she admitted.

"I'll have to remember that." Shade tucked the hefty folder under his arm and placed his free hand in the small of Lori's back to steer her toward the door. "It's a habit I got into when I was married. Vicky had to have someone make all the decisions."

Lori didn't want to talk about Vicky Ryan. She let Shade guide her ahead of him and waited while he turned out the lights and closed the conference-room door. "What time should I be there? Where is the presentation?"

"I'll pick you up. If that's all right with you?" Shade grinned. "See? I'm learning."

When Lori was standing in the bathroom a half hour later, she realized that her smile was a mirror of the one she'd seen on Shade's face. Although she usually looked forward to quiet evenings, she found herself anticipating the prospect of seeing Shade again. It was the idea of learning more about the timber industry, she told her reflection, but even she couldn't ignore the skepticism in her eyes. A slide show had nothing to do with her mood.

Lori showered and shampooed and even found the patience to use a hair drier on her short curls until they floated instead of curled around her ears. She had almost talked herself into a sweater and skirt outfit when she spotted the soft pink crepe dress she'd bought for a party Brett insisted they attend. She'd only worn the expensive garment once. It didn't make sense not to let it see more service. Besides, she admitted once she'd cinched up the contrasting hot pink belt, *my boss deserves to see me in at least one dress.* The soft, puffy three-quarter-length sleeves and full skirt draping gently around her hips made her feel more feminine than she had in years. If only she had some perfume or jewelry to go with it. But her few pieces of jewelry were still packed away, and she hadn't bothered to buy perfume for a long time.

That was because there hadn't been anyone she wanted to get close enough to to give off a message of femininity for a long time.

Not tonight, old girl, Lori told herself before snapping off the bathroom light. *Tonight isn't for gnawing over old bones.* Tonight she was going to a slide show with Shade Ryan.

THE SLIDE SHOW represented a trip down memory lane for Lori. She was surprised by the turnout for the program, held in a converted ballroom managed by the historical society. As they were waiting for the program to begin, Shade explained that in addition to a notice placed in the local paper, announcements of the show had gone out to senior-citizen groups, the woodworkers' union and the schools. "Despite the advent of the computer, this is logging country. People remember what it was like when the men in the family started working in the mills as soon as they were out of school. Besides, if you don't mind my tooting our horn, the historical society has a reputation for putting on a quality program."

Lori couldn't have agreed more. Even with Shade

sitting next to her in the crowded room, she half forgot where she was and whom she was with. As she was shown a pictorial history of the progress of logging operations since earliest times, she found herself viewing the slides through her father's eyes. He might make a few minor comments about some of the points the narrator was making, but Lori was sure he'd agree that a fair portrayal of the industry was being made.

Her eyes grew misty as they were shown logging camps in the middle of the wilderness that consisted of nothing except tents and small trailers. Lori had spent time in more than one of those camps. As a small child, she knew almost nothing about the world of city apartments, department stores or schools with different teachers for each grade. It seemed incredible that she had grown up far removed from experiences most children took for granted, but because she hadn't experienced hot-lunch programs, shiny yellow buses and educational specialists, she didn't miss them. Her upbringing was unique, not inferior.

Shade remained detached from the presentation. He couldn't shake the impact of the presence to his right, a slim arm brushing against the sleeve of his velour pullover. Occasionally, he glanced at her, trying to picture the petite woman clamoring over the clear-cuts, running down logging roads, watching her father prepare a meal in the most primitive conditions. Although a protective streak in him wanted to deny that she probably knew more about the sights and smells and sounds of what they were seeing than most of the people here, he was able to acknowledge the impact this upbringing had had on her. Lori Black was, if nothing else, a product of her childhood. Learning more about that product was a lesson he was eager to begin. Hard as it was to sit next to her and not touch her, he could acknowledge that pushing a physical relationship might ruin a more permanent one. *Don't close yourself off from me,* he asked silently. *I need to reach you.*

As the show ended, the lights came on, and people started getting to their feet. Lori was aware of how many people stopped by to talk to Shade, but she continued to sit in her hard-backed chair, thinking. Even when she'd been thrown into a college environment, she didn't think of her earlier years as something that would be recorded for posterity. One-room schoolhouses, a person's belongings piled into the back seat of an old car, a father with pitch on his hands and wanderlust in his soul—those were the things that added up to what she'd become.

"Are you all right?" Shade asked, his hands lightly on her shoulder.

"What?" Lori blinked and looked up. "I was just thinking about my father. You know, sometimes I was the only child in one of those logging camps. How many men would be able to raise a child by himself under those conditions?"

"It really was as bad as the slides showed?"

"Complete with tents and water that had to be trucked in." Lori smiled at the memory. "It takes a long time for the twentieth century to reach the mountains. My early education was patchwork to say the least."

"I wonder if that's the best way for a child to be raised."

Lori drew away. "Shade, it was the only thing I knew. I can't remember ever wanting to fight the way I lived. I always had books. I learned a great deal that way."

"But you weren't around other children." Shade helped her to her feet. "I'd think that would bother your father."

"Black Bob didn't have much need for people. He raised me the same way." Reluctantly, Lori allowed Shade to lead her from the room. Although she was becoming more aware of the man guiding her, she was reluctant to leave her memories. "I just wish Black Bob could have been here tonight. He'd enjoy it." She laughed softly. "Of course he wouldn't have much use for a roomful of people. He'd probably bolt before the program was over."

Shade wrapped his arms around her, holding her against his strong, warm body. He wouldn't let her do the same! The emotion was so intense that it rocked him. "You didn't bolt," he said, trying to comfort himself. "Maybe you two aren't from the same mold, after all."

No, I didn't, Lori admitted to herself. She remembered how uncomfortable she used to be when Brett dragged her to one public gathering after another. She hadn't felt that way tonight. She might have tried to tell herself that she had lost herself in the presentation, but that would have been a lie. It wasn't just the material being presented that allowed her to sit comfortably in a roomful of people; this man had played a crucial role. "I wish you could meet my father," Lori whispered against Shade's chest. "He's one of a kind."

Lori felt Shade's lips brushing across the top of her head, and then he spoke. "I would like to meet the man who raised such a beautiful daughter. Come on. Let's get out of here."

With Shade running interference, they were able to leave the still-crowded building. Lori didn't ask what he had in mind as they got into his car and left the parking lot. Shade had called her beautiful. She'd have to remember to wear a dress more often.

"What did you have for dinner?" Shade asked once they were alone.

Lori had to think before she could answer him. "Soup," she said, laughing. "Out of a can."

"What am I going to do with you? You can't earn your salary if all you eat is soup. I know a place that sells the most spectacular and fattening milk shakes you've ever seen. Do you want yours with or without whipped cream on top?"

Lori tried to object and tell Shade that he'd already done enough for one evening, but he refused to listen to her. "When I decide to pamper a woman, the least she could do is accept gracefully," he pointed out. "You can worry about dieting tomorrow."

Lori gave up. The truth was that she wanted to be with Shade. After the evening they'd shared, the house on the hill would feel empty. Shade pulled into the small, neat ice cream parlor and ordered for both of them. They chose a corner table and attacked their tall frosty glasses. "I love these things," Shade said around a full mouth. "I have to go to so many meetings planned by little old ladies who serve sandwiches that wouldn't fill a squirrel. I'd much rather come in here and pig out."

"Why do you go to those meetings?" Lori had to ask. "I mean—if you don't like them."

"We all have to do things we don't like. Look, I like people. I also have times when I need to be alone. Or with just one person. Like you." Shade stopped eating and met Lori's eyes. "I'm not going to pretend you're nothing more than another employee. I'm not sure what it is, but I want to be with you."

"I'm flattered," Lori managed. She was glad he'd said that and wanted to acknowledge his honesty. "I'm not much good at the art of small talk, I'm afraid."

"That's what I like about you. You say what you want to, not what you think you should be saying. Does Black Bob get credit for that?"

"I guess. He certainly is a maverick."

Shade smiled and touched the tip of her nose the way he had the night he'd fixed dinner for them. "I wouldn't call you a maverick. In fact, I don't know what label to paste on you. You don't fit into any mold."

Lori flushed and turned her full attention to her milk shake. "I don't know what to say," she managed.

"But you can admit that. Don't you see? A lot of women feel they have to cover up, make some remark that spoils the mood. Oh—" Shade frowned. He hadn't wanted to say what was going to come next, but if he waited much longer, he would probably talk himself out of it. "I almost forgot to tell you. Vicky might be coming back earlier than I expected."

"Should I move out?" Lori took another swallow of milk shake, but the cold concoction seemed to have lost its appeal.

"No." Shade touched her hand as a way of reinforcing his statement. "When she called, I told her someone was house sitting. She isn't sure she wants to come back to the house, anyway. If only she'd make up her mind!"

Lori started, unprepared for Shade's anger. "Why is she coming back early?"

"Who knows?" Shade forced himself to take a calming breath before continuing. He hadn't wanted to mention Vicky tonight, not only because it was Lori he wanted to think about but because thoughts of his ex-wife still confused him. "Who knows what that woman is thinking about, ever. I'm sorry. I don't mean to drag this out around you, but it makes me so damn frustrated that she can't make up her mind about anything."

"Are you sure it's her fault?" Lori asked, aware that she might be treading on dangerous ground. "I mean, you said she was pretty young when you got married. She hadn't had much chance to be on her own. You made all the decisions in your marriage."

"I didn't have much choice," Shade explained. "You want to know how bad it was? If it had been her I'd taken to the slide show, I'd have to make the decision on what she should wear. What kind of woman can't decide what she wants to wear?"

Lori didn't have an answer for that. She wanted to tell Shade she didn't want to talk about his ex-wife. But Shade was obviously on edge. Now wasn't the right time to say something that might upset him more. And really, she couldn't blame Shade. A man might not mind helping his daughter choose her clothes, but a wife should be capable of making those minor decisions. As she thought about it, it seemed remarkable that Vicky was able to face the fact of being divorced at all. "Shade?" she ventured. "Who wanted the divorce?"

Shade looked at her, his expression saying that was the last thing he expected. "Both of us. Maybe Vicky more than me."

"Why?" Now it was her turn to touch his hand, a comforting gesture, she hoped. "I mean, Vicky depended on you so much."

"I know." The words were a deep whisper. "But

neither of us was happy. I knew I wasn't helping her stand on her feet, but I didn't know how to go about doing that. I was willing to hang in there, be her prop. But—'' Shade stared without seeing for a minute. ''But I have to hand it to Vicky. She knew I wasn't happy the way things were going. She said she didn't want to hold me back anymore.''

''She asked for the divorce?''

Shade laughed bitterly. ''Not exactly. She started talking to this friend she's on tour with. The friend got her lawyer to contact Vicky. I understand now that a lot of what was holding Vicky back was uncertainty about her financial future. Because of a lawyer—who probably bought a new car, thanks to me—Vicky got the security she needed. Damn. How did we get on this subject?'' As if to put an abrupt end to it, Shade got to his feet and stood at the door, waiting for Lori to join him.

On the way home Lori concentrated on the sharp, steep turns, trying not to glance at the stony profile next to her. This wasn't the way she wanted the evening to turn out. It had been so long since she'd felt like spending time with a man. It wasn't fair to have Shade's past come between them. He was obviously in no mood to come up with any small talk, and it was too late for her to start learning that art.

To her surprise Shade walked with her to the door and came in after she'd unlocked it. ''You wouldn't happen to have any decaffeinated coffee, would you?'' he asked.

''Don't you have to go to work tomorrow?'' Lori frowned. She shouldn't have said that. She didn't want him to leave. ''You're going to be tired,'' she wound up.

Shade sighed. "I'm going to be tired whether I stay here or go home. I'm not going to be getting much sleep. Unless—unless maybe you rather I leave?"

Lori glanced up at Shade, caught the shadows around his jade eyes and shook her head. *Don't leave, please,* she thought. "No. Of course not. I'd like to share some coffee with you. Maybe you'd like to choose some records. I really enjoyed the ones we were listening to the other night."

"You can play any of them you want to," Shade said, turning toward the living room as Lori headed for the kitchen.

A few minutes later Lori had coffee brewing and joined Shade in the living room. She could sense his need to spend time with his thoughts, but that didn't make it easy for her to dismiss the fact of his presence. They sat in silence, glancing through the evening paper, Lori distracted. Finally, her restless squirming caught Shade's attention. "You are tired. Why didn't you tell me?"

"Because I wouldn't be a very good hostess. Honest, I'm not tired. I don't mind." It was true. The shadows had been lifted from Shade's eyes; she much preferred sharing the room with him to being alone. "I don't think I thanked you properly for the evening, or the milk shake. It was fun."

"It was, wasn't it." A slight, grateful smile touched Shade's mouth. "We'll have to do that sort of thing more often. Look, forget the coffee. It's more important that you get your sleep."

He was going to leave. No! Lori scrambled to her feet and hurried to the kitchen. "I'd be offended if you left without sampling some of my coffee. I want you to know I really can cook. At least I can boil water."

Shade's laugh accompanied her on her journey and surrounded her mind as she filled two mugs with steaming coffee. Shade was standing by the sliding-glass door, looking down at the valley lights, when she handed him his mug. "I can't believe how much I love this view," he said softly, his free arm coming around Lori and holding her so she could appreciate the same thing. "In the winter, when it's too cold to sit outside, I slide my chair next to the glass so I can still see out. Or at least that's what I used to do."

Lori took a long, relaxing breath and leaned her body against Shade's strength. The lamplight at the opposite end of the living room did little to disturb the night that had crept in through the glass. Steam from the coffee was warming her hand and face. Warmth from Shade's side and arm was completing the glow spreading through her body. "I think you need to move back here," she said softly. "Maybe Vicky would let you have the house."

"Maybe. I didn't think so a few weeks ago because of the memories, but the house feels different now, better." He turned toward her. "You're the difference. You've brought new life to the house." He hadn't meant to say that much. The realization that Lori's presence had gone a long way toward erasing the memories that went with the house was something he was willing to admit to himself, not Lori. But the words were out, and now that they were, they'd become something he had to acknowledge. His hand tightened around her, allowing him to draw from her. Maybe it wasn't wrong, after all. Lori was a woman who, he believed, was ready for honesty in all its forms.

Lori didn't dare return Shade's gaze. She had no idea how it had happened, but in the space of a heartbeat, warmth had turned into heat. Shade's arm became charged with a sensual brand of electricity that was consuming her. The alarming thing about that was that she wasn't sure he was aware what he was doing to her. "I—thank you," she managed weakly.

"You're welcome. You're shaking. Are you cold?"

Lori gripped her coffee mug tightly. Not cold. Something much more dangerous. Flames had reached her inner being, her very core, it seemed. She sucked in air through her nostrils in a desperate attempt to regain control of her emotions. "It must be because I'm tired," she lied. "I feel a little shaky."

Shade's lips were on her temple, light feathers of electricity that were nearly Lori's undoing. "Maybe this will help. Did I tell you how much I enjoyed tonight?"

"I think you did." He had to realize that there was a direct route from her temple to her breasts, that her nipples had hardened and were straining toward freedom. She could only hope he wouldn't press the point.

"But not the way I want to," Shade was saying. He pulled the mug out of her nerveless fingers and laid it on a table next to his. "You were the most beautiful woman there tonight. I want to tell you that. Every time I thought about the way you looked, I forgot what it was we'd gone out for."

She hadn't been aware of that, not at all. She'd been so caught up in memories of her father and childhood that she hadn't thought that much about Shade. That had all been changed now that they were alone and he'd put his arm around her.

This time his touch wasn't the companionable gesture it was a minute ago. Shade took her neck between his hands, his fingers spread to stretch from her ears to her collarbone. He was gazing down at her, eyes dark and intense.

Lori shuddered. Her legs were weak, so weak that she swayed. She wanted to lift her arms to clutch him in support, but they were too heavy. All she could do was stand where she was and gaze up at eyes that captured her every thought.

Their kiss was so gentle, so reverent, that it cooled a little the intense emotion that consumed her a moment ago. Their bodies barely touched, but Shade's hands on her neck held her as securely as the most ardent embrace. Lori leaned toward him, a willing participant in their mutual experiment.

Her eyes closed slightly; she could see that his eyes were open but hooded. Her lips acknowledged the fact that he was smiling.

"That was nice," Shade whispered. "Chaste but nice."

"Thank you, sir," Lori managed, grateful that he wasn't expecting more in the way of speech from her.

His eyes never left hers as his fingers trailed lower on her collarbone, found the soft boat-neck dress top and started to explore the flesh under the pink fabric. Lori opened her lips slightly as the need for more oxygen grew. His fingers were on the swell of her upper breast, stopped from further exploration by taut fabric. Knowing that he wanted to explore more, but was unable to, added to her sense of the forbidden. They shouldn't be doing this. He was her boss.

No. That didn't have anything to do with tonight, not really. They were both adults, unmarried, free to do whatever they wanted.

And Lori wanted Shade's hands on her body, his lips

touching hers. She hadn't felt that urgency for a very long time, maybe never.

The next time Shade lowered his head to touch her lips, she found the strength she lacked a moment ago. Her arms went around his waist. She was the one with the need to press their bodies together, to feel his muscular legs against her thighs, to know the mixture of pleasure and wanting that came from experiencing the layers of fabric separating their flesh. Shade placed his arm around her back and pressed her breasts against his chest. Lori didn't try to keep her eyes open. His body felt even harder than it looked. He was a rock, a mass of granite that formed the perfect contrast to her own slight frame.

So this was what was good about being small and slight. For maybe the first time in her life, Lori found nothing wrong with her soft womanly body. Maybe it wasn't capable of doing all the physical chores she wanted from it. But it was perfect for molding against a man's body.

Their kiss became more than a tentative exploration. Lori parted her lips, delighted because Shade was doing the same thing. Shyly, she explored the opening with her tongue, delighting in the feel of his teeth, his tongue. If speech hadn't been impossible, she would have told him that he was tickling her.

Shade's hands left her waist and traveled upward to the top of her zipper. She shuddered as she was freed and his hands were free to explore her backbone, the angles of her shoulder blades. "You're so soft," he whispered around their sealed lips. "Soft and yet strong under that softness."

That's the way I want to be for you. Lori's thoughts went no further than that. She no longer was asking herself whether this should be happening. The experience consumed her. She allowed Shade to push her away from him long enough to pull the dress off her shoulders, but before he could unfasten her belt, she pressed her breasts against him again, needing the contact.

It felt awkward but very sensual to be kissing a man with her dress half off, bunched around her waist, while her shoulders were naked except for her bra straps. The night air was igniting the downy hairs on her shoulders, but next to the greater impact of feeling his heart beating against her breasts, the slighter sensation was lost.

Shade covered her shoulders with his hands. His lips left her mouth and sought the side of her neck. Lori arched her head away from him to give him greater access to the long, slender line. She was aware of her body's slight trembling and nearly cried out with the wonder of what was happening to her.

The thought of how completely Shade was able to control her body frightened her. Before this moment they'd only shared a short, chaste kiss. Now his fingers were lifting the straps on her bra, reaching for the firm mounds that ached for his touch. They were going too fast. Too much was happening.

"Shade, I—"

"I know," he groaned, bringing his hands back to safer territory. "Don't say it. I'd better leave."

Don't! Don't leave me wanting you like this. "I think that's best."

Shade pushed her abruptly away from him and turned toward the door, groping for the door like a blind man. "I hope you don't regret this. I didn't know it was going to happen, but I'm not going to apologize."

"I'm not, either." How she'd found the strength to speak she didn't know. "Drive carefully."

She was alone. The heavy front door was between her and the man who'd left her with her dress only half on. For a long minute Lori stared at the door before looking down at herself. The top of her dress was a jumble of fabric held in place by the hot-pink sash belt. Her shoulders were coming alive with goose bumps that had nothing to do with cold air.

Lori started to lift the fabric back in place until she realized it didn't matter. Instead, she unfastened the belt, pulled it free and let the dress slide off her hips.

She turned toward the bedroom without bothering to pick up the dress.

Chapter Six

No matter how many times she'd seen it done, Lori still cringed when limbs were being removed from trees that had been growing for decades. She turned from the work being done on the oak nearest the house and bent over to pick a sprig from a mint plant. She crushed the sprig between thumb and forefinger and brought her finger to her nose, relishing the fresh, alive aroma. The limb had to go. It grew so close to the roof that in a wind branches scraped the old shingles. And yet Lori felt as if she were condemning the proud old tree to something it would never ask for.

Ruth was seated at her usual place inside the screened porch, enjoying the activity, although nervous about machinery so close to her rose garden. Lori picked another mint sprig and brought it with her for Ruth's enjoyment.

"It's really something," she said as she sat near Ruth. "The truck-mounted lift they have for high work is much safer than having a man climb the tree and try to remove a limb by himself."

"I hope he knows what he's doing. If they damage any of my roses—"

"I told them they'd have to answer to me," Lori

reassured Ruth. She was glad Ruth was outside. During the first two days of the week Ruth hadn't felt up to leaving the house. "With both of us keeping an eye on them, they're going to be extra careful. Here." She gave Ruth the mint. "I thought you'd enjoy this."

Ruth smiled and crushed a leaf to expose the aroma. "I love mint. My husband thought it was a waste of time to plant mint, but then what does a man know about such things?"

Lori nodded in understanding. "I agree. It takes a woman to appreciate certain smells. Well, what do you think of what's been going on here lately? Things are really looking different, aren't they?"

Ruth nodded, her body relaxing a little. "I talked to Shade on the phone yesterday. He called to see how I was and what I thought of the tree trimmers you'd hired."

"Shade was checking up on me?" Just speaking Shade's name did things to Lori, but she was upset by the implication in Ruth's statement.

"Of course not, my dear," Ruth reassured her. "But Shade knows how I feel about the farm. I'm sure he was just making sure I wasn't having second thoughts about putting the farm in the society's hands. I wouldn't have done it if I didn't know how sensitive Shade is to such things. He's such a considerate man."

"I agree." Lori kept her eyes resolutely on the work being done. She hadn't seen Shade for nearly a week, but he'd had to be out of town for a couple of days, and she'd decided to spend the weekend exploring several of the small towns in the eastern part of the state. Now it was Wednesday, and her commitment to the farm and Shade's need to catch up on work at the museum hadn't left room for anything except a couple of telephone calls. Just the same, she didn't doubt that Ruth could look into her too-big eyes and know that something had stirred her emotions.

"Shade said he'd try to come out here and have lunch with me," Ruth was saying. "I invited him, but he said he'd accept only on the condition that he bring lunch. That's what I mean about his being considerate. He knows it's harder for me to whip up a meal than it used to be."

"Ruth," Lori ventured, "have you been to a doctor lately? You just don't seem to have the color you did the day I met you."

"A doctor isn't going to do me any good, my dear," Ruth said emphatically. "What's wrong with me is I'm looking at ninety years of age damn soon. My body's getting tired."

"Maybe. But—"

"Don't you bother yourself with me," Ruth interrupted. "You can worry about being old when it happens to you." She turned her attention back to the workers. "That limb's just about off now. I certainly hope it misses the house when it comes down."

Lori had been assured that the arborists were professionals, but she couldn't sit where she was while the workman pulled on the rope around the limb. Not that her presence would assure safe removal, but at least she'd feel better if she could see what was happening. She gave Ruth a reassuring grin and stepped outside.

To her relief the men managed to bring the limb crashing to the ground on the driveway, expertly missing the roof and shrubbery around the tree. She gave Ruth the thumbs-up signal and went over to the foreman to discuss removal of another limb. As they talked, Lori rolled up the sleeves of her cotton blouse and pushed her hair away from her forehead. It was a warm spring day, and the breeze was barely moving.

By the time she saw Shade's car coming down the driveway, Lori's hair was clinging wetly to her temples. She'd lost all interest in the bag lunch waiting in her Mustang. She waved at Shade but didn't feel comfortable leaving the work being done. It was probably just as well. Telephone calls had been relatively safe. How she would react when he was close enough to allow her access to his eyes was something she wasn't sure she was ready to test.

It seemed only a few minutes before Shade was getting back in his car. This time he stopped near the center of activity and got out of his car. "Things going okay? You missed a succulent lunch. Hamburgers and root beer."

"That's what you brought Ruth? You're a real gourmet," Lori chided him. She had never felt this alive simply from being close to a man before.

Shade shrugged, obviously unconcerned. "Ruth doesn't get out to many fast-food joints. I thought she might enjoy it. I was right. She ate all my fries. How about you? Have you had lunch yet?"

Lori leaned against the tree surgeon's truck and pushed her hair off her forehead with an irritated gesture. She gave herself a mental shake, trying to free herself of Shade's impact. "I'm too hot to be hungry. Rain a few days ago and now this warm spell. Things are growing like crazy."

"Mushroom weather." Shade's voice took on a wistful tone. "Do you know how long it's been since I've gone mushroom hunting?"

"Years? At least that's how long it's been for me.

Shade?" Lori frowned. "I'm worried about Ruth. Her color doesn't look good to me. Have you noticed?"

"She's unsteady on her feet. She doesn't want to admit it, but it's hard not to notice. I'm trying to get her to see a doctor." Shade joined her by the truck, giving her a playful shove with his hip so she would make room for him. "I hope I won't have to start worrying about two women. Will I have to stay here to make sure you get something to eat?"

"In a few minutes." Lori breathed deeply. She wasn't about to tell Shade what she was feeling, but already her heat-induced exhaustion had been replaced by one of increased sensitivity because their hips were touching. "I'm glad you found time to come see Ruth. She thinks a lot of you."

"I think a lot of her, too. Did you enjoy your weekend? You like exploring, don't you?"

Lori nodded. She'd taken two rolls of pictures during the weekend, probably to the puzzlement of the residents of the sleepy little towns she'd wandered through. "It's that old wanderlust of mine. I love exploring new places."

Shade's finger reached out and laced with hers. "I hope that doesn't mean you're going to be gone every weekend. I missed you."

I missed you. "I didn't want to drag you around with me," she explained. "I figured you had better things to do. Not everyone likes to wander around back roads."

"Next time ask me. I know you like being alone, but I don't think it would hurt to try sharing yourself with someone once in a while."

Lori was aware of the deeper emotion beneath Shade's words and wondered if he was criticizing her.

The question was on Lori's lips, but the feel of his fingers intertwined with hers stopped her. He wouldn't be holding hands if he was angry with her. "I didn't think," she admitted. "I'm just used to doing things on my own."

"Next time ask." Shade gave her a quick peck on the forehead before releasing her hand. "I'm sorry. Duty calls. What do you know about morels?"

Lori's words were tinged with memories. "You're asking a mountain girl what she knows about morels? They're best fried in butter."

"I knew there was something special about you." Shade winked. "Fried it is. It just so happens that I know a spot about five miles from here that should be alive with them after that rain. How—" Shade drew out the question. "How would you like to go hunting with me?"

"Don't!" The thought of covering a steak with fresh morel mushrooms brought Lori's appetite back full force. "How can I force down a sandwich after you've dangled that in front of me?"

"I thought you knew. I'm a sadist. Tonight, after work. I'll call you."

He was gone. Lori stared at his retreating figure, not trying to deny how much pleasure it gave her to watch the smooth play of muscles as his thighs moved within their linen covering. She wasn't ready for the emotion. After feeling so little in a marriage bed, she was reacting strongly to the simple act of a man walking. At least he couldn't know how deeply she'd been touched by the simple prospect of spending several hours wandering through the woods looking for mushrooms. That was an act from her past, touching base with what had given her childhood meaning.

Lori distracted herself by tackling her uninspired lunch and then pushing the workmen along to make sure they completed work on two other trees before quitting time. They probably thought her an unrelenting taskmaster, but she had to be accountable to the society's financial director. Besides, working at full speed gave her little time to wonder what the evening might bring. She'd lost count of the times she'd gone mushroom hunting with her father, but tonight would be different. She'd be with Shade, insulated from the world by the woods they'd be in.

She had just stepped inside Vicky's house when the telephone rang. "I'm still at the museum," Shade explained. "But I should be out of here in five minutes. What if I pick you up at your place? I don't suppose I have to remind you to wear boots."

Lori glanced at the kitchen clock. "I'd really like time for a shower," she explained. "Otherwise, I'm not going to be fit to be with."

"If you'll wait, I'll wash your back for you."

Lori laughed and hurried into the bathroom as soon as she'd hung up. She fully intended on taking a quick shower, but as soon as the cool spray hit her, she knew there was no way she was going to be able to jolt her tired body into action. She took a long time shampooing her hair and then stood with her face lifted under the faucet before soaping her body. She'd probably have to take another shower tonight to protect herself against any poison oak they might come across, but she needed this to revive herself. She was out of the shower but wearing nothing except a towel when the doorbell rang.

"I'm in the bathroom," she called out. "Come in. There's ice tea in the refrigerator."

She heard the door open and close and turned back to the task of drying her hair. She thought about throwing on some underwear, but the effort seemed overwhelming. Maybe she should tell Shade she was too tired for anything. She would have if he'd suggested anything except the chance to relive a treasured childhood memory.

The bathroom door opened. A hand holding a glass of wine worked its way through the crack. "This was in front of the iced tea," Shade deadpanned. "You are one slow woman. I thought you'd be ready by now."

Lori held on to the top of the towel wrapped around her with one hand and accepted the wine with the other. "I can't seem to get moving." She smiled, decidedly nervous at the thought of having to share the bathroom with a fully clothed man, especially this man. "The humidity today really sapped me."

"A hike will revive you, if the wine doesn't put you to sleep first." Shade's eyes glinted with amusement. "Is that what you're going to be wearing?"

"Will you get out of here?" she ordered with mock severity. She couldn't order a man out of what was in reality his bathroom. "I can't get dressed with you in here."

"You should have thought of that before you invited me in." He leaned against the now-closed bathroom door and folded his arms across his chest, the gesture making his upper arm muscles bulge. "I'm afraid you have an audience."

"And I'm afraid you're going to be disappointed." Lori took a sip of wine, hoping that her outward calm was enough of a camouflage for what she was feeling inside. "I'm not going to get dressed with you standing here."

"I don't mind." Shade's eyes slid slowly down her

body. "That outfit will do just fine. The skirt's a little short."

Lori warned herself not to look down, but even as she was forming the words, she glanced at her legs. The towel barely reached the top of her thighs. "You're embarrassing me," she admitted.

"I'm honored. I haven't embarrassed anyone for a long time." Shade's eyes closed to slits. "I don't recall anything in your contract that protects you from being seduced by your boss. In fact, I'm going to add that clause if it isn't in there already. Besides, I can always claim you enticed me by your attire, or rather lack of attire."

"You're the one who walked in here."

"Minor point. They'll never hang me with that evidence."

In less time than it took for Lori's heart to beat once, Shade reached out and touched the top of her towel. A single yank and it would have been stripped from her. Instead of taking advantage of the situation, Shade turned around and started out the bathroom door. "Hurry along, woman. I'm starved," he called over his shoulder.

Lori slammed the door behind him and leaned against it, too surprised to do anything except laugh. At least she no longer felt too tired to move. She wondered at the self-control that kept him from stripping her and admitted that knowing that about him made him even more special than he was already.

Five minutes later Lori was wearing a man's shirt, faded jeans and comfortable walking boots. She was still lifting her short curls with her fingers as she walked into the kitchen, an empty wineglass in her free hand. "There," she said. "Is that better?"

"You expect me to give you an honest answer? Can

you guess what I really wanted to do?'' Shade asked. He started to refill her glass before she could object.

Lori didn't know what to say. She accepted the glass and took a sip, more to have something to do than out of enjoyment of the wine.

"I'm serious,'' Shade continued. "I've been doing things around you that I didn't ever think I'd do. I keep telling myself I'm your boss. I have no business unzipping your dress or—"

I haven't told you to stop. "Maybe we need to have a lawyer write up a contract,'' Lori said out of a need to fill the silence. "He can tell us what is and isn't acceptable behavior in our situation. I'm not much help. I haven't had much experience in this sort of thing.''

Shade sighed and downed his wine. "I should know better. Come on. Let's get out of here before I do something else I'm going to have to apologize for.''

If you apologize, I'll have to, too, Lori thought as they went through the front door together. *I look at you and see muscular thighs, shoulders like a mountain, a broad chest. That isn't what an employee is supposed to see in an employer.*

Because she saw Shade glancing at it, Lori suggested that they take her Mustang. She settled into her seat with a couple of plastic bags for collecting morels on her lap, her mood quickly joining Shade's as he reinforced the need for secrecy about where they were going. "We can't be too careful about this,'' Shade pointed out, his eyes on the rearview mirror as if on the lookout for someone tailing them. "I found out about this place from a logger friend. He'd been in there clear-cutting about three years ago. Wouldn't have told me if I hadn't bribed him with a beer or two.''

"We used to post guards when we were stalking morels," Lori said, joining in the spirit of their adventure. "I've heard of people who are willing to kill for information about a prime site." She sighed. "It's been so long. I've almost forgotten how much I enjoyed doing this with Black Bob."

"You'll enjoy doing it with me." Shade was almost to the bottom of the mountain, but instead of heading into the valley, he took a country road that took them into the hills to the west of town. After about five miles he turned off onto a gravel road that soon faded away to a deeply rutted dirt road. Before Lori could become concerned about her car's ability to straddle the ruts, he pulled off to the right and got out.

"End of the road. Now we start hoofing."

Lori fell in line behind Shade as he plunged into the thick shrubbery that nearly covered a thin trail. "Black Bob and I knew a man who swore the only time you could hunt mushrooms was at dawn," she told his back. "I was always a little leery of him, but Black Bob and he got along just fine."

Shade stopped and turned back toward Lori. "Do you always call your dad Black Bob?"

"Most of the time," she admitted. "He said I started doing that when I heard the other loggers call him that. He thought it was cute."

"Hmm. Unique man, your father." Shade resumed plunging through the bushes. "I'd like to meet him."

"I want you to," Lori said with more feeling than she thought would come through. Her father enjoyed the company of men like himself but had always drawn inside himself when required to rub shoulders with men who didn't make their living in the woods. She wondered what Black Bob would think of Shade.

"Have you noticed anything different about Ruth

lately?" Shade asked, breaking through her thoughts. "She doesn't seem as interested in teasing me as she used to."

Lori fought her way back to the here and now. Although the question was important, it still seemed rather inconsiderate of Shade to interrupt her thoughts. But what he was saying was something that had to be discussed. "I think you're right. She should see a doctor," Lori said. "I haven't known her very long, so I can't make much of a comparison, but she doesn't have much zip these days. You know what I think? I think living alone in that old house, taking care of it, is getting too much for her."

Shade leaned forward, walking slower now. "Do you think she should go to a nursing home?"

"Oh, no!" Lori was surprised that Shade would even mention such a thing. Ruth loved her home as much as Lori loved the wilderness. Denying either of them their beloved environment would be a death sentence. "Don't do that to her, Shade. Don't even think it. I know she's turned her affairs over to the historical society, but don't take away what makes living worthwhile to her."

"Then what do you suggest?"

"Maybe a housekeeper," Lori said, her thoughts barely keeping pace with her words. She wasn't out of breath, but she did have to concentrate on where she was walking. "I haven't given it enough thought. But maybe that's the answer. If she had someone staying with her—"

"I don't think so," Shade interrupted. "You're the one who said it. The farm is what makes life worthwhile for her. She'd never agree to sharing her home with a stranger."

"It wouldn't be as if we threw some strange nurse in with her," Lori protested, all too aware that an easy solution wasn't forthcoming. "We'd have to give the two women time to get to know each other, decide if they could get along."

"When you've been alone and independent as long as Ruth has, it isn't easy," Shade pressed. "Go ahead. Make the suggestion if you think you have to, but I don't think it's going to work."

"I will," she said firmly. "I'm willing to try anything short of a nursing home. That's where people go to die."

"It all depends on how you look at it," Shade said over his shoulder. "One thing that bothers me about having Ruth stay where she is, even with a competent housekeeper, is that the stairs are still there. If she fell and hurt herself— She'd be a lot safer where facilities are planned for the safety of the patients."

"Ruth isn't a patient. She's a delightful old dear who deserves happiness in her last years."

"Not if independence is going to endanger her life. Look, you don't like the idea of a nursing home. Maybe that wasn't a wise choice of words." Shade paused a moment. "How about one of those retirement facilities, those apartments people can buy into that have housekeeping services and medical staff on hand."

"You're still not getting the point." Lori tried to keep her voice low, but it wasn't easy. "Ruth has lived her whole life on that farm. Uprooting her now would kill her."

"You'll never know unless you try. Keeping her where she is might kill her. Look, I know all about your damned independence, and I know that one of the things I did wrong is overprotect Vicky, but this is different.''

Shade's words stopped Lori for a moment. There was no denying that Ruth could injure herself in the old house. But forcing her to live jammed up against people she didn't know in a sterile apartment wasn't the answer, either. "I don't have any answers," Lori said softly. "All I know is, it would kill me if I had to live in one of those places. Some people simply aren't made for living elbow to elbow with others.''

"What about my elbow? Do you mind that?''

Lori frowned, trying to keep up with the new direction the conversation had just taken. "Are you trying to change the subject?'' she challenged.

"You noticed. We're here.'' Shade stepped to one side so Lori could join him. "I just wonder how you feel about having me around all the time.''

Lori didn't answer. Instead, she allowed herself to be distracted by her surroundings. They'd been walking along what remained of a skid road, but now the terrain had opened up to reveal the results of a recent clearcut. Poking up from the stubs of trees felled by the logging crews were new seedlings. The seedlings were dwarfed in size by the brush, now exposed to the sunlight, but in a few years the carefully planted trees would be the first to be touched by a morning sun.

Lori breathed in the scent of what was as familiar as breath itself to her. It was true that she enjoyed her own company and relished the hours of solitude. Having Shade enter her world and wanting to be part of his world was calling for adjustments she wasn't sure she could handle. She failed, miserably, with her husband. Right now, maybe because being with Shade was a new, heady experience, she was eager to share this experience with him instead of being alone.

But she didn't know if it would last. Lori once thought she'd be able to be a wife. She'd turned her back on the quiet voice that rebelled against a man's intruding on her private space, taking away the quiet that was part of her background.

She was wrong. Marriage wasn't what she thought it would be. There was too much togetherness, too much probing into her privacy. She didn't know if what she felt for Shade was different enough or if she was heading toward those same feelings again.

"I like having you around." Lori laughed, striving for a light tone. Not tonight. She wasn't going to think heavy thoughts tonight. "Who else provides me with a beautiful house to live in and takes me mushroom hunting and gives me a job?"

"You're just after my money." Shade's face fell in mock soberness. "I should have known." If Shade was aware of what she was trying to sidestep, he wasn't mentioning it.

"That's it," Lori quipped back, relieved that Shade wasn't pressing his earlier question. She handed him one of the plastic bags and started toward a rotting log that might be housing the highly prized mushrooms with their distinctive pits and ridges running in all directions. "When I saw the size of your wallet—"

Shade headed toward a tree stump. "Strange. I wasn't carrying a wallet that first night out at the farm." His voice softened. "What I remember is a beautiful young woman with wet hair stringing around her face and a shirt so soaked it left nothing to the imagination."

Lori blushed, but because her back was to Shade, she didn't think he'd notice. "I'm sorry. I wasn't thinking about that."

"I know." Shade dropped to his knees and pinched off a three-inch morel at the base of its white stem. "That's what I found so intriguing. You had no idea what you looked like. You didn't seem to care whether I was a rapist or a robber or anything. You were so trusting."

Lori snipped off a morel of her own with her nails and dropped it in her sack. "That's what Brett used to say. He said I was too trusting. Maybe that's what comes from growing up the way I did. There weren't many people around. Dad and I got to know the ones we were around pretty well."

"I better remember that. Lori, someone needs to take care of you."

I don't need anyone to take care of me, Lori thought. *I've never needed that.* "The only thing I need out of you, Shade Ryan, is for you to keep a rash promise you made in a moment of weakness," Lori challenged, because they'd come too close to something dangerous in their relationship and she needed to shy away from it.

"Me? A rash promise? I don't believe it."

Lori nodded somberly, or at least she hoped she was being somber enough. To her relief, Shade seemed willing to leave serious discussions behind. "You made a couple of disparaging comments about my car. Something about the brakes, if I remember. Are you going to recommend a good mechanic?"

"I'm a good mechanic," Shade boasted as he dropped several more morels in his bag. "And it wasn't just the brakes. I could name a half-dozen things that car needs. There are certain responsibilities that go with being en-

Shade?" Lori frowned. "I'm worried about Ruth. Her color doesn't look good to me. Have you noticed?"

"She's unsteady on her feet. She doesn't want to admit it, but it's hard not to notice. I'm trying to get her to see a doctor." Shade joined her by the truck, giving her a playful shove with his hip so she would make room for him. "I hope I won't have to start worrying about two women. Will I have to stay here to make sure you get something to eat?"

"In a few minutes." Lori breathed deeply. She wasn't about to tell Shade what she was feeling, but already her heat-induced exhaustion had been replaced by one of increased sensitivity because their hips were touching. "I'm glad you found time to come see Ruth. She thinks a lot of you."

"I think a lot of her, too. Did you enjoy your weekend? You like exploring, don't you?"

Lori nodded. She'd taken two rolls of pictures during the weekend, probably to the puzzlement of the residents of the sleepy little towns she'd wandered through. "It's that old wanderlust of mine. I love exploring new places."

Shade's finger reached out and laced with hers. "I hope that doesn't mean you're going to be gone every weekend. I missed you."

I missed you. "I didn't want to drag you around with me," she explained. "I figured you had better things to do. Not everyone likes to wander around back roads."

"Next time ask me. I know you like being alone, but I don't think it would hurt to try sharing yourself with someone once in a while."

Lori was aware of the deeper emotion beneath Shade's words and wondered if he was criticizing her.

The question was on Lori's lips, but the feel of his fingers intertwined with hers stopped her. He wouldn't be holding hands if he was angry with her. "I didn't think," she admitted. "I'm just used to doing things on my own."

"Next time ask." Shade gave her a quick peck on the forehead before releasing her hand. "I'm sorry. Duty calls. What do you know about morels?"

Lori's words were tinged with memories. "You're asking a mountain girl what she knows about morels? They're best fried in butter."

"I knew there was something special about you." Shade winked. "Fried it is. It just so happens that I know a spot about five miles from here that should be alive with them after that rain. How—" Shade drew out the question. "How would you like to go hunting with me?"

"Don't!" The thought of covering a steak with fresh morel mushrooms brought Lori's appetite back full force. "How can I force down a sandwich after you've dangled that in front of me?"

"I thought you knew. I'm a sadist. Tonight, after work. I'll call you."

He was gone. Lori stared at his retreating figure, not trying to deny how much pleasure it gave her to watch the smooth play of muscles as his thighs moved within their linen covering. She wasn't ready for the emotion. After feeling so little in a marriage bed, she was reacting strongly to the simple act of a man walking. At least he couldn't know how deeply she'd been touched by the simple prospect of spending several hours wandering through the woods looking for mushrooms. That was an act from her past, touching base with what had given her childhood meaning.

new, heady experience, she was eager to share this experience with him instead of being alone.

But she didn't know if it would last. Lori once thought she'd be able to be a wife. She'd turned her back on the quiet voice that rebelled against a man's intruding on her private space, taking away the quiet that was part of her background.

She was wrong. Marriage wasn't what she thought it would be. There was too much togetherness, too much probing into her privacy. She didn't know if what she felt for Shade was different enough or if she was heading toward those same feelings again.

"I like having you around." Lori laughed, striving for a light tone. Not tonight. She wasn't going to think heavy thoughts tonight. "Who else provides me with a beautiful house to live in and takes me mushroom hunting and gives me a job?"

"You're just after my money." Shade's face fell in mock soberness. "I should have known." If Shade was aware of what she was trying to sidestep, he wasn't mentioning it.

"That's it," Lori quipped back, relieved that Shade wasn't pressing his earlier question. She handed him one of the plastic bags and started toward a rotting log that might be housing the highly prized mushrooms with their distinctive pits and ridges running in all directions. "When I saw the size of your wallet—"

Shade headed toward a tree stump. "Strange. I wasn't carrying a wallet that first night out at the farm." His voice softened. "What I remember is a beautiful young woman with wet hair stringing around her face and a shirt so soaked it left nothing to the imagination."

Lori blushed, but because her back was to Shade, she didn't think he'd notice. "I'm sorry. I wasn't thinking about that."

"I know." Shade dropped to his knees and pinched off a three-inch morel at the base of its white stem. "That's what I found so intriguing. You had no idea what you looked like. You didn't seem to care whether I was a rapist or a robber or anything. You were so trusting."

Lori snipped off a morel of her own with her nails and dropped it in her sack. "That's what Brett used to say. He said I was too trusting. Maybe that's what comes from growing up the way I did. There weren't many people around. Dad and I got to know the ones we were around pretty well."

"I better remember that. Lori, someone needs to take care of you."

I don't need anyone to take care of me, Lori thought. *I've never needed that.* "The only thing I need out of you, Shade Ryan, is for you to keep a rash promise you made in a moment of weakness," Lori challenged, because they'd come too close to something dangerous in their relationship and she needed to shy away from it.

"Me? A rash promise? I don't believe it."

Lori nodded somberly, or at least she hoped she was being somber enough. To her relief, Shade seemed willing to leave serious discussions behind. "You made a couple of disparaging comments about my car. Something about the brakes, if I remember. Are you going to recommend a good mechanic?"

"I'm a good mechanic," Shade boasted as he dropped several more morels in his bag. "And it wasn't just the brakes. I could name a half-dozen things that car needs. There are certain responsibilities that go with being en-